Death of a Sunday Writer

Death of a Sunday Writer

Eric Wright

Thorndike Press • **Chivers Press**
Thorndike, Maine USA   **Bath, England**

This Large Print edition is published by Thorndike Press, USA and by Chivers Press, England.

Published in 1997 in the U.S. by arrangement with W.W. Norton & Company, Inc.

Published in 1997 in the U.K. by arrangement with HarperCollins Publishers Ltd.

U.S. Hardcover 0-7862-1198-9 (Cloak & Dagger Series Edition)
U.K. Hardcover 0-7540-3097-0 (Chivers Large Print)
U.K. Softcover 0-7540-3098-9 (Camden Large Print)

The text of this Large Print edition is unabridged.
Other aspects of the book may vary from the original edition.

Set in 16 pt. Plantin by Minnie B. Raven.

Printed in the United States on permanent paper.

British Library Cataloguing in Publication Data available

Library of Congress Cataloging in Publication Data

Wright, Eric, 1929–
    Death of a Sunday writer / Eric Wright.
       p. cm.
    ISBN 0-7862-1198-9 (lg. print : hc : alk. paper)
    1. Women detectives — Ontario — Toronto — Fiction.
2. Large type books. I. Title.
    [PR9199.3.W66D45 1997]
    813'.54—dc21   97-24774

A Dedication
To the staff of
Peterborough Public Library

Acknowledgment
Grateful thanks are due to Howard Dover
for his help and advice.

Chapter 1

The note Lucy Brenner found on her desk when she arrived at the library that morning said that Walter Buncombe had called and left a Toronto number for her to call him back. Lucy recognized the handwriting of her boss and looked up to find the chief librarian watching her from across the room. "He didn't say what it was about," Janice Waller said. "Don't you know him?" she added to an obviously puzzled Lucy.

Lucy shook her head, and now the other two librarians looked up. " 'A Gentleman Caller,' " pronounced Jocelyn Thomas, the children's librarian. She had been a librarian for thirty years. Facetious by nature, very early in her career she had developed the habit of speaking in titles.

Lucy dialed the number and the voice of a secretary responded, gabbling the name of a company. Lucy asked for Walter Buncombe.

"He's in a meeting. Would you like to leave a message?"

Lucy identified herself. "I'm returning his

call," she said. "Who is he?"

"Mr. Buncombe?"

"Yes. Who is he? What does he do? Who are you?" Lucy's favorite television programs had been interrupted several times recently by people who wanted to sell her something on the telephone, and she was now practicing being aggressive to all telephone callers who did not identify themselves sufficiently.

The other librarians were now sitting back in their chairs, frankly listening.

The secretary's voice said, "Mr. Buncombe is a partner here."

Lucy asked, looking round at her colleagues to include them in the conversation, "Partner in what? And where is here?"

"This is the office of Buncombe and Hart."

"Who are Buncombe and Hart?"

"This is a legal firm."

"So he's a lawyer."

"He's a *partner*."

"What does he want me for?"

"I really couldn't say. I'll leave your message, shall I?"

"Yes. I'm here until five. Tell him to keep trying." She hung up. "Some lawyer in Toronto wants me," she told the others.

"Ah," they said, more or less collectively, and went back to work in case the word

8

"lawyer" meant that Lucy after all had a problem that she would not want to share further.

Lucy wondered first if her estranged husband had finally decided to institute divorce proceedings. But he had asked her again to return to him only the week before, so what could have happened to change him? Her thoughts ranged back over the last few days, looking for any other bad news that a lawyer might have for her. Was her neighbor suing her to get the fence fixed? Could she have been in an accident she wasn't aware of, a parking lot encounter, or brushed aside one of those mothlike old ladies who teeter fragilely on the curb in your blind spot when you are making a turn on a red light? But that would be the police, surely?

While she was wasting her time wondering, the lawyer called again. She confirmed that she was Lucy Brenner, and then, mysteriously, who her grandparents had been. The lawyer said, "I am calling in connection with your cousin, David Trimble."

"I can't help you, I'm sorry," Lucy said quickly. "I haven't seen him for years, not since my grandmother died, and I never knew anything about him. Nothing at all."

Buncombe said, "I'm not looking for him. I am, or was, his solicitor. I'm sorry to tell you he died yesterday."

"I see. Thank you for calling."

"Hold on, Mrs. Brenner. You are named in his will. You're his sole surviving relative. His heir."

This was more interesting. "Did he leave an . . . estate?"

"Legally, that's what it's called. But it didn't amount to much, I'm afraid. The furniture from his office and his apartment, his clothes, a few hundred dollars. A few other personal effects."

"Nothing valuable, then? I'm not rich?" She looked round at her colleagues to signal them that they could once again listen in.

The lawyer laughed. "David never had any money."

"Did he die . . . ?" She wanted to say "easily." Trimble's death meant nothing to her, but he was a human being and she hoped that his end wasn't painful or tragic.

"A heart attack. Quite quick."

"I see. Well, now you've found me, I presume you can send me anything that's left over. Or do I have to arrange the funeral?"

"No problem. He left himself to a hospital."

"I see. Thank you very much, then."

"Mrs. Brenner, I'm also calling to ask if

you would take care of his personal effects. It would be easier than bringing in a dealer. And you would get what value there is."

A phrase came into Lucy's head from a Barbara Pym novel, a sign on the side of a truck: DECEASED'S EFFECTS REMOVED.

Would she be able to find someone in the *Star*'s want ads to remove her cousin's effects? "You mean, come to Toronto?" And as she said it, the problem became an opportunity, the possibility of a diversion. "When should I come?"

"Could we do it tomorrow?"

"What time?"

"Eleven?"

"I'll probably have to stay over." She glanced across the room and got a nod from the chief librarian to make whatever arrangements she had to.

"There's a cheap hotel on Church Street. I could get a room for you, if you want," Buncombe was saying.

"Good. Yes. Where is your office?"

He told her.

"Can I park nearby?"

"There's a lot opposite the office."

He had missed the point. Park free, she meant, in one of his company's spaces, not for three dollars a half-hour. "All right. Eleven o'clock, then." She put down the

11

phone and looked at the calendar on her desk.

Lucy worked part time at the main branch of the Longborough library on an hourly basis, and it was no great inconvenience to anyone for her to take a day or two of unpaid leave. She had no other arrangements to make, no young children, no animals, or birds, or tropical fish — nothing except a phone call to postpone an appointment with a man who was coming to look at her furnace. Mrs. Tusker, next door, would keep her porch free of junk mail in exchange for the gossip about her cousin's death.

The other librarians were waiting now to find out who had died.

"My cousin," Lucy said. "I'm his heir."

They watched for their cue to see how they should react.

"We had the same last name before I married, but I hardly knew him."

"Ah," the women said in unison again, lightly.

"Still . . ." Jocelyn Thomas said, her voice full of speculation. " 'A Woman of Property.' "

"He died broke. The lawyer wants me to sort out the bits and pieces. He wants me to go in tomorrow."

"Do you mind?" Bunny, the reference librarian, asked, now that they had all adjusted to the size of the news. "Sort of ghoulish."

"No. No. It won't be . . . sad, will it? Might be interesting."

Now the other women put aside the last traces of any attitude of condolence they had assumed. "There's a sale on at IKEA," Mrs. Waller said. "Take your time. We can manage."

They could manage for a week if necessary, Lucy thought. She worked, more or less at her own speed and in her own hours, on nonurgent but necessary tasks, mainly in the basement workroom. "Let's say three days, for now." She remembered something. "I'll have to come back the day after tomorrow, though. I'll let you know what's happening then."

Chapter 2

That night, as she tried to sort out the clothes she would need for three days in Toronto, Lucy recognized that after two years of freedom, she still hadn't solved the problem of a wardrobe she could forget about.

She had left her husband after a twenty-three-year marriage. The preparations for leaving had been long and difficult. For the first eighteen years there had been a child to worry about, a daughter, but when Jill moved out to British Columbia to take a course in dental hygiene, and stayed out West after graduation, Lucy was left alone to realize that now she might do something about the fact that she had been miserable for a very long time.

At first, of course, she had to work through all the guilt and the sense of failure that came with admitting the truth. Her ancestors included generations of farmers, people who regarded unhappiness as a moral defect as long as you had enough to eat and no one was hitting you. She had succeeded in concealing the reasons for her unhappiness from herself for twenty years, assuming that it was her fault, and that it was in her power to find satisfaction within her circumstances, or change those circumstances by taking evening courses, enrolling for volunteer work, and yoga as soon as she had time. But when she began to investigate the opportunities after Jill left, she found that every initiative was blocked, and she could no longer avoid seeing that her problem was her husband.

From the very beginning of their marriage he had discouraged her from having any other interests but him. At first his attitude seemed to be that the two of them were self-sufficient, that outsiders were a nuisance, and he paid such close attention to her, calling her several times a day from his office, and arranging outings and "treats," like weekends in Vermont, that she assumed that marriage was like that. When Jill came along, the child became an extra reason why they were too busy to bother having people to dinner, or to go to parties. In a few years she had no friends and almost no outside interests, but she did not realize then that that was the condition he had been working toward.

The daughter, Jill, might have created the

spark of revolt, but she was timid by nature and encouraged in her timidity by the fence that her father built around the family. What saved her was her failure to get a place in a dental hygiene program close enough to home so that she could continue living with her parents. Her father tried to make her change her choice of career to one that she could train for in a local community college, but the suggestion was a mistake because it allowed Jill a first clear glimpse of where her father's advice was coming from, his need to keep her locked in the tower. She grew up on the spot, insisting on following the career of her choice.

She came home once a year, and on her last visit had quarreled with her father. The quarrel began with a fairly harmless comment from her about family relationships, some small psychological commonplace she had picked up on the West Coast, which sent her father into a towering rage, a rage that once would have silenced her, but now had her shouting back at him. She went back to Victoria a day early. Since then, mother and daughter had talked on the telephone, and several times Jill had hinted she would be glad to see her mother, alone, in Victoria for a visit. It was no more than a suggestion; the two had never had a chance to become allies, and Jill could have no idea how close to a crisis her mother was. Jill felt rather than thought, and after the quarrel she felt sorry for her mother. But Lucy, bred to be loyal to her spouse, did not yet encourage her.

After Jill had gone, when there was both the time and the need to enlarge her space, and she began to look about for something to do, something to study, or just to know about, Geoffrey brought a noisy mockery to bear on all her attempts to rediscover the world, and she saw finally that she was married to someone whose need to keep her dependent on him would close every window. He had become her jailer.

She avoided seeking professional help at first because, she guessed, if Geoffrey found out, he would respond negatively and violently to this, too, suspecting a criticism of their relationship and thus of him (like Jill, she had begun to get an idea that Geoffrey's attitude grew out of some psychological deformity in himself that he was refusing to know), but she read in a newspaper of a profession called "lay therapist" or "counselor" for emotional problems, and decided that would do. Geoffrey was no more in touch with contemporary trends than she was, and if he asked she could tell him she was getting treatment for her back.

So she took the first step, small, but in her case momentous, the step of finding someone to talk to. In half a dozen conversations in which the therapist said hardly a word, she came quickly to the truth, and she began to look for the means of escape. Looking back later, she realized that her misery had ended as soon as she had made the decision to leave him, and in the final stages of her marriage she was nearly content in the knowledge that at the right moment she would go.

Thus there was nothing unusual about Lucy's situation, except that Geoffrey had been so successful in keeping the world away from her that she was late in waking up. Eventually the means of escape arrived, in the form of a legacy from her mother, enough money to buy a house, and she began to plan. On a hint from her therapist, she put the money in the hands of a respectable lawyer (in the teeth of Geoffrey's assumption that he was the proper person to manage it) and waited. She stayed another year, propped up by the knowledge of her nest egg, seeing Geoffrey increasingly more clearly. Then one afternoon the moment came, and she packed a bag and called a cab.

She never went back. A week later she had a part-time job in the library in Longborough, a town halfway between Kingston and Toronto, and two months after that she opened a guest house offering bed and breakfast, an enterprise from which she earned enough, with her part-time job, to make her feel secure. She had been living in Longborough for two years now, steadily getting stronger, preparing herself, though she hardly knew it, for the next move in her progress away from being Mrs. Brenner. By way of a hobby she had suggested herself as the editor of the library bulletin, and even wrote one or two paragraphs of library news for the Longborough *Examiner*. There were still many times, especially on Sundays, when she felt very lonely; sometimes she felt that she had not only left Geoffrey behind but a whole other life, as if she had emigrated to a country where she knew no one, but the mood was more of a luxurious melancholy than the nagging misery she had felt in Kingston. Like many emigrants, she had exchanged the despair she had felt at home, more acute because she was at home and therefore trapped in it, for a much more bearable loneliness, more bearable because it was only to be expected under the circumstances, not really her fault. By supper time it was gone, dissolved in the anticipation of Miss Marple, or better yet, Inspector Morse. Even on the rainiest Sunday afternoon, she never doubted that she had made the right move, finally.

Packing for an overnight trip confronted her with some problems with her wardrobe that she had long been avoiding. After she moved to Longborough, Lucy had made a determined effort to remain open to experiences in every area of her life, to say yes to anything short of shoplifting. She tried to dress less sensibly: She wanted strangers to wonder who she was, and what she did for a living. She bought herself a pair of athletic walking shoes, like Minnie Mouse boots made of rubber, and then, for the same reason — because she no longer had to defend her choice to her husband — she came home from a shopping expedition with some khaki culottes, a yellow waistcoat, and a white silk blouse with gigantic sleeves. She might have managed each item separately but she made the mistake of putting them all on together, along with the walking shoes, and felt like a middle-aged clown, and wondered if it wasn't all too late for her. Next, she toyed with an image of herself in a huge skirt and with purple, cable-stitched stockings and flat shoes, a costume that would have given her an intellectual air and allowed her to wear her hair in its natural condition, a frizzy tangle of almost-gray, but decided that such outfits look best on thin women, and while Lucy wasn't fat, she certainly wasn't ethereal.

She tried the L.L. Bean look — loafers, corduroy pants, and a checked shirt, and this worked at the library but not in the evenings, even in Longborough, and so she stayed with her old wardrobe until she could acquire some clothes-education. She did buy a trench coat that made her feel independent and was fine as long as it looked like rain, but underneath she had not yet found a solution.

Now she assembled a gray flannel pleated skirt and two blouses, which she would wear with the top button undone and a necklace of pieces of blue lapis-type rock. Some progress was made: In the course of sifting through her jewelry she did finally throw out her wooden beads and the stainless steel clip in the shape of a giraffe, items she occasionally put on in despair, but that always made her feel glum by the time she got to work. Looking at her wardrobe, she felt she ought to have made more progress with it, and away from the Kingston she had fled nearly two years before, and she determined to look round the shops in Toronto.

Chapter 3

The trip marked the first time that Lucy had driven to Toronto alone. Always before, even when she had been the driver, she had an acquaintance, usually another librarian, riding shotgun, as it were, someone who had grown up making the trip to the metropolis whenever something major had to be bought, or to see one of the extravagant musicals that had taken over Toronto in the last few years. Now, for the first time, she was her own navigator, and she had worked out a route very carefully, writing out the directions in block letters on a sheet of paper she put on the passenger seat so that she could read it at any pause in traffic: Along the 401 to the Yonge Street exit, then south to Canadian Tire, left along Davenport to Church Street, then south all the way to Colbert Street. She arrived in a light sweat from trying to read the names of cross streets while navigating the closely bunched traffic, but when she braked, finally, and switched off, she felt that another small hurdle had been jumped.

★ ★ ★

The legal firm of Buncombe and Hart occupied offices in a small warehouse that had been scraped back to its original brick and converted into professional suites. A tiny freight elevator took Lucy up to the third floor, where she walked round a corridor full of graphic design consultants until she came to the lawyers' sign. She introduced herself to a woman behind the counter who shouted, "Wally!," then pointed over her shoulder for Lucy to go into a back room. Buncombe opened his door and waved her in, a telephone receiver clamped under his chin. Lucy shook the dry old hand that Buncombe was holding out, and sat down.

"There'll be a counterclaim if you try that," Buncombe said, and put the phone down. He studied Lucy for a few moments, then said, "He wasn't a fine man," crouching down with the air of someone about to attack, making his statement sound like a password, requiring a specific response.

Lucy tried to remember if there was any context for the statement in their telephone conversation of the day before.

Buncombe remained crouched, but he now had on a little smile. She looked appropriately puzzled, and Buncombe roared with laughter and stood up. "I was just getting

24

rid of the preliminaries. You didn't know him, did you? Not for years, you said."

"Wasn't he a fine man? He *is* dead." Her cousin's naming her his heir made her want to defend him.

Buncombe was unabashed. "He was a scamp."

"He was a crook?" This was interesting.

"David Trimble was *bad*. Just legally and morally. Wouldn't hurt a fly unless the fly had pockets."

"A thief?"

"Not that." Buncombe smiled, looked at her under thick white eyebrows, rolled his eyes round the room, doing a "guess-again" routine, and waited. He made a silent word with his lips.

"What?"

He shook his head, then uttered the word. "Horses," he whispered, and winked.

"He was a gambler?"

"And he knew bad people. Took chances."

"He *was* a crook."

"Never caught."

"Was he a thief, a gangster, an arsonist? What?"

"No, no. Just the gee-gees."

"But he didn't win much, according to you."

"About six hundred in the bank. He didn't even own a car.

"A good thing he left himself to the hospital. Where is he now?"

"The morgue."

Lucy began to wonder if all of Buncombe's clients suffered, as she was suffering now, from his conversational style, and if so, whether he charged by the minute. He seemed to say nothing naturally; everything was delivered for effect, as if it was profound or hilarious. Lucy occupied the time in the dramatic pauses and the explosions of mirth by wondering why his wife didn't make him trim the hair that sprouted, uncontrolled, from his ears and nostrils.

It took some time for him to tell her that her cousin had died of a massive heart attack. Someone across the street had seen him lying on the floor of his office. The body was still warm when the police arrived. A routine autopsy had followed, and the pathologist reported that Trimble's heart was in a very dilapidated condition. He was lucky to have lived so long. There was no need for any further investigation.

"Nothing else? No insurance?"

"Nothing else. Just his furniture and a little computer."

"What about the business? Is there any

26

goodwill? What was his business?"

Buncombe started as if he had been lightly pricked. "Didn't you know?" He paused. "Didn't I explain?" Another pause. "Surely I mentioned it?" An even longer pause. "No?"

Lucy was tempted to say, "That's right. You did. I forgot," and walk out, but she wanted to know. She shook her head.

"Gumshoe!" Buncombe said, doubled-up, in hysterics. "Gumshoe! Private detective! Not a very good one, though, judging by his bank account. He spent more time with the gee-gees than he did working."

But Lucy wasn't listening. Gumshoe. To one who had found her escape from the world of Geoffrey Brenner in the world of mystery novels for the last twenty years, the very word was like a spell. She would have guessed that David Trimble imported string, or registered trademarks. This was worth any trouble her cousin would cause her, just in terms of the story she would be able to take back to Longborough. And perhaps there was more to this than just a good story.

"What kind of gumshoeing did he do?" she asked.

"Watching." Buncombe threw himself below the level of the desk until only his eyes

27

were visible, moving from side to side, acting out the word.

Lucy's irritation, her need for a bit of plain speaking, drifted across the desk.

Buncombe stood up, sad at the lack of applause. Now the tone of his voice suggested incredulity that she should require any amplification. "He watched people. I gave him one or two jobs and referred him to clients who had simple jobs they needed done. Sometimes someone is needed to watch someone's comings and goings. If you think your husband is having an affair with a friend of yours, you might have someone like David watch the house, her house, for a few nights."

"Did he tail people?"

"Follow them, you mean? I don't think so. He wouldn't have been much good at that. A bit overweight." Buncombe bubbled slightly, but controlled himself. "He just sat in a car in the street for fifty dollars an hour and took pictures of people going in and coming out of the door he was watching. The trouble was, as I said, David didn't even own a car, or rather he owned a lot of cars but none for very long, so when he got a job he usually had to rent one. He only worked when he had to, and he wasn't, very, good." Buncombe emphasized all of the last three words equally, ending in a shout of laughter as if he had just expounded the most extraordinary paradox.

Lucy was forced to smile slightly, or appear rude. "He must have been some good at picking winners, then."

"Not even that! He lived hand-to-mouth, just holding his own." He opened a drawer. "Now, here are the keys to his office and his apartment. And there's a package at the morgue." Buncombe slapped the keys on the desk in front of her.

Lucy looked at the tag on the office keys. "Egerton Street. Where's that?"

"South off Queen, between Bathurst and Spadina."

"And the apartment? Fortescue Road?"

"Off Bloor Street, near Bathurst."

Lucy put the keys in her purse. "You say he actually named me in his will?"

"He made it early last year. At the time, he still had a bit of the money his mother left him — that's all gone now — and I was trying to get him to put something away for his old age. I like all my clients to make a will: People who die without a will create problems for us all. So he told me to go ahead, and when we looked for a legatee, he said there wasn't anyone except you. He remembered that you'd invited him to your wedding."

"I'd forgotten." An image of a jaunty little man in a bright green tie floated to the surface.

"He hadn't. Gamblers are very sentimental about things like that. I did a search and found that you were running — a hotel? — in Longborough."

"A bed-and-breakfast."

"He liked the sound of that. He talked of looking you up, but then he thought that if he died, it would be a pleasant surprise for you, so to speak."

"What a nice idea. He might have won a lottery in the meantime, then I'd be rich."

"He didn't, and you're not."

"He tried, though, didn't he?" Discovering you are liked by someone you are hardly aware of is always pleasant. "And if I have any other questions?"

"Just call. I won't charge for a phone call."

Chapter 4

She walked through to Market Square to find a cup of coffee while she decided what to do. The restaurants she passed all seemed to be assuming it was lunchtime, but she wasn't yet hungry so she bought coffee from a take-out shop and found a seat on a bench in the little park opposite the St. Lawrence Centre.

So far her inheritance had provided a small, interesting outing. Now she had to dispose of her cousin's effects, and go back to Longborough. She wondered if, in arranging to stay overnight, she hadn't made too much of the expedition. Longborough was only a hundred and fifty kilometers away, and some people there commuted to Toronto daily. But if she stayed here, at least for a night, she could try to find some clothes. Surely there would be something in the Eaton Centre.

She sat in the park for half an hour, drinking her coffee, acknowledged by no one except an old tramp to whom she gave a quarter. In Longborough a dozen people would have greeted her by now, and she smiled at the irony. When she had moved to Longborough in the first place she wanted the world to evaluate her afresh, separate from the assumptions that were involved in being Geoffrey Brenner's wife, but she had not been allowed to remain a stranger long once the librarians had understood her situation. It was slightly exhilarating to be once more anonymous.

She dropped her paper cup into a wastebasket and looked at the address that Buncombe had given her. She would still have preferred to leave her car in the lot and take the Queen streetcar. But now that she had driven through the city once, it seemed feeble, and the car would certainly save time.

David Trimble's office was one of a number of cubicles above a row of small stores at the corner of Egerton and Queen Streets. As Lucy started down the gloomy hallway, looking for the name, a door swung open at the far end and a policeman came out, followed by another man, a middle-aged Oriental — a well-groomed, athletic-looking man wearing bifocals, and dressed in a gray sweatshirt and baggy pants.

"I'll arrange for a padlock until we find

out who owns this stuff now," the policeman said. "Can I help you, ma'am?"

"I'm looking for David Trimble's office."

"You've found it. Who are you? What do you want with him?"

"I'm his cousin. I came to clean out his office."

"Somebody already did." The policeman pushed open the door and stood back for her to look in.

The office had been wrecked. All the desk drawers were upended. The contents of a filing cabinet had been dumped out. A box of computer paper had been emptied on the floor. The little computer itself looked undamaged, though the monitor had been lifted off the drive unit. A few books had been taken out of a bookcase and lay about the floor.

"I understand your cousin died," the policeman said.

Lucy nodded. "Burglars?"

"I guess. Young kids looking for cash, I would think. Real crooks usually take stuff like that." He pointed to the computer. "Have you been in here lately?"

"I've never been here before. I haven't seen my cousin for twenty years."

"In that case you won't know if anything is missing. I understand he died of a heart

33

attack just recently."

"So I was told." She looked around at the mess. "I should report this, shouldn't I?"

"He already did. That's why I'm here." The policeman nodded toward the Oriental, who put out his hand. "Peter Tse. T-S-E, pronounced 'See.' "

"The janitor?"

"This is my building. I own it."

"I'll go back and make my report," the policeman said. "You'll want some time. I was going to padlock the office. The lock is busted. You want me to do that now, still?"

"Yes, please," Lucy said. "How long will it take?"

"I'll have the guy in the hardware store downstairs come right up." He walked off, down the corridor.

Lucy had no idea what to do next. Peter Tse followed her into the office. "Pretty bad," he said. "A bad mess. But I don't think they got anything." He smiled companionably and sat down.

"How do you know?" Lucy walked over to the window that looked out on Queen Street, resenting very slightly the way Tse had invited himself in. He had an odd but faintly familiar accent, certainly not Canadian, probably Hong Kong or somewhere like that.

"David never had anything. He borrowed fifty dollars from me the day before he died. He always owed me fifty dollars. And sometimes the rent, too."

"I'll settle his debts as soon as I can," she said over her shoulder. She wondered if she was being conned. It seemed an easy way for the landlord to pick up fifty dollars.

Tse stood up and carefully placed his chair behind the desk, then dusted off his hands. "I didn't say that because of that. I don't mind fifty dollars. I just said that because you asked what they got. You think David might have had some money? He never had money. These toughs just broke in to look for things to steal. I don't mind fifty dollars. I liked David. So I lent him fifty dollars. Okay?" He turned toward the door.

"I'm sorry. But what about the rent?"

"It's all paid up until the end of the month. He paid the first and last month's rent and he is one payment behind, so at the end of the month it's finished."

"I have two weeks to clear this out, then?"

"All the time you want." He walked out, leaving the door open.

Lucy righted a second chair, sat down, and pressed her hands between her knees. She had been rude to that Chinese man, because she was nervous. He was just trying to be helpful.

The man from the hardware store appeared and screwed on the hasp for a padlock. She paid him and added the keys to her ring, then looked round for a point to start cleaning up. She had just refolded the computer paper when Peter Tse appeared in the doorway, which she had carefully left ajar.

"I'm sorry, Mr. Tse," she said immediately. "I didn't mean to sound rude."

Tse looked at her through the top of his bifocals, his head down. Satisfied, he smiled. "Yes, you did. And now you're sorry. Okay. You look hungry. You want to come and eat with me?"

This was sudden. She had no Chinese friends in Longborough, but there was a mythology about the men, she remembered reading somewhere. They found middle-aged Caucasian women irresistible. No, they found them disgusting, smelling of milk products. Either way, it didn't matter at noon on Queen Street, west of Spadina, surely. "I wouldn't mind a bowl of soup," she said.

"Let's go. He put on your lock? Let's go."

He shepherded her along the corridor and down the stairs out on to the street, and into a Portuguese coffee shop. While she drank her soup and he ate some dark gray fish, Tse talked. First he established that she did not know her cousin or anything about him. Then he explained.

"David was . . ." he paused, searching for a word. "Bad," he concluded.

A scamp, she remembered. "Why?"

"He knew some bad people. They came to his office. Betting people."

"He was a private detective. He was bound to have bad people among his clients." It was something she probably knew more about than he did, in theory at any rate.

Tse laughed. "He didn't do much detective stuff. Mostly betting."

"But he did have some clients."

"A few. Not too many. He didn't work very hard on the detective stuff." Tse continued to grin at the idea of Trimble, the detective.

"If he borrowed the rent from you, he wasn't a very good bettor, either, was he?"

"Sometimes. Sometimes he won. Sometimes he paid me two or three months' rent. Other times I lent him a few dollars."

"Why?"

"I liked him. He was a bad bugger, but a nice man."

"How was he . . . bad? Was he swindling people?"

"Oh, sure. I don't know who, though. He was a swindling type of man. I think he worked for bookies, too."

"How?"

"He helped them find people."

"What kind . . ."

"People who don't pay. When he found them, the bookies made them pay." Tse nodded several times to emphasize the words.

"You mean he was an enforcer?"

Tse roared. "David couldn't enforce a duck. No, he found the people, then the enforcer came."

"How do you know?"

Tse showed his teeth. "People have told me they've recognized some of the ones who come to David's office."

"Do you think the bookies or the enforcers could have been the ones who broke into the office?"

"Why? No. That was just toughs. Kids. Why would bookies break into David's office?" He was genuinely puzzled.

"I don't know. That policeman thought it was kids looking for money. But maybe it was someone else. Do you know what case David was working on when he died?"

Tse grinned. "I don't think he had any *cases* lately." His emphasis was derisive. "He's been in his office a lot lately, reading, playing with the computer."

Lucy said nothing.

"What are you going to do?" he asked her.

"Clean up the office, I guess. Find a way to get rid of the stuff."

"I'll clean up for you. I'll buy his stuff. I've got tenants want a chair or a desk."

"But then . . . oh, no." Lucy was looking forward to finding out about her cousin, having a good poke around his private life, but she couldn't say that to Tse. "No, that's my job."

"Okay. If you want to sell anything, though, maybe the computer, I'll buy it."

"I'll have to see."

She worked steadily through the afternoon. The phone rang twice for her cousin; both callers rang off immediately at the sound of her voice. At the end of the day she felt she had properly sorted the mess into two discrete piles. There was the material that seemed to have come out of the desk drawers. Most of this had to do with horses. There were pictures of horses, old clippings of accounts of major races, race programs, guides to making money by gambling. There was some clean underwear, two laundered shirts, socks, toothpaste, combs, a pair of hairbrushes, a bottle of cologne from Trumper of London, a pair of reading glasses.

The pictures that had been pulled off the walls were also of horses, and as the afternoon wore on, Lucy began to get an impression of her cousin. Within the limits of his fluctuating income, he was a dapper dresser who affected a British "Members' Enclosure" style of costume, and was obsessed with horses, not just with betting. There was evidence — some pictures, a book on equitation — that at some earlier, and probably lighter, period Trimble had even tried to ride.

From the filing cabinet she learned that his last case as a private detective was apparently three years before. Each case was recorded on a single sheet of hand-written paper in a file folder. There were fifty or sixty such folders. She pointed this out to Tse on one of the many occasions that he put his head round the door to see how she was getting on.

"Try the computer," Tse said. "After he got the computer he put everything on it. I told you, he never stopped playing with it, moving paragraphs, stuff like that."

40

Of course. She reserved the computer for later.

At six, Tse appeared again, and she asked him how to get to Trimble's apartment.

Trimble had lived in a building south of Bloor Street, near Honest Ed's; she found her cousin's name among the tenants listed in the basement. A brief look around the tiny "studio" apartment told her that it was no more than a camp. There was a single bed, an armchair, a television set, and a kitchen table and chairs. Mostly there were clothes, slightly horsy jackets, an off-white raincoat of a military type, and even an old pair of riding boots. It seemed a sound idea to call the Salvation Army to cart it all away.

By the time she had finished looking around, she was hungry, and she walked back up to Bloor Street, where she had noticed on some of the side streets people sitting outside, eating at not-very-expensive-looking cafés, the sort of places where she could have some supper and watch the people on the street. She found a café in the next block that had an awning over the sidewalk and took a table. Although Kingston was only two hundred and fifty kilometers away, she had hardly visited Toronto for the last fifteen years because Geoffrey could not see the point. Now, sitting out on the sidewalk eating shepherd's pie washed down with a glass of wine made her feel that she might be anywhere. Amsterdam, perhaps, or Malmö.

Chapter 5

That night, in her hotel room, she set about listing the errands for the next day. She still had to pick up Trimble's personal effects from the morgue. That, disposing of the office and apartment furnishings, and seeing Buncombe for the last time should do it. Her enthusiasm for her little outing was ebbing. Eating supper outside had been the high point of the day; being alone in a small, cheap hotel room in downtown Toronto was less fun than she had thought it might be. After supper she had driven back to her hotel and then gone for a walk. She had a glass of wine in a bar on Front Street where the thumping music and bad light had made it impossible to read her book, and now she wanted to talk to somebody, to be among familiar surroundings, at home in Longborough.

She found herself reminded of those first bad days after she had left her husband, and felt a mild panic. She was confused, now, because she thought she was well past the panic stage. She felt sufficiently free of Geoffrey that she had even told him where she lived in Longborough, and he had visited her several times, always hoping she would be ready to return to him, but each time he looked a little stranger, more unfamiliar. Inevitably, then, she had progressed from feeling secure to feeling restless, as if life in Longborough was not the end after all, but the beginning of the road outside the prison gates. And yet now, on her first outing to Toronto, she was scared again, having to remind herself that the first day of anything was always like this.

And then she remembered that The Trog was coming the following night. He had called the day before, from Baghdad, it sounded like, judging from the background noise, and the idea of him cheered her up enough to send her to sleep.

The next morning the city looked friendlier, and she had a good poke around the Market area, a much renovated part of downtown that smelled of French coffee and hot bread at that time of the day. (She chose the Market café for her own breakfast, though, because it looked like a Longborough diner and she wanted a bacon sandwich.) She window-shopped for an hour and, by the time she was ready to go back

44

to Trimble's office, felt altogether better about her expedition and reluctant to abandon it so soon.

Her landlord was waiting for her at the office. She had the impression that Peter Tse spent most of his time gossiping around his building, but at the same time she was very glad to see him.

"You had a visitor," he said from the doorway, before she had switched on the light. "I told him to come back."

"Did he say who he was?"

"No."

"Did he ask for me or David?"

"He said anybody would do. He asked if you would be around today."

"Did he look like a bad man?"

Tse grinned. "No. Maybe a little bit."

"When's he coming back?"

"Eleven o'clock."

She looked at her watch. It was ten-fifteen. "I'll wait here, then. I still have a few things to do here. Don't go far away, will you?"

"I'll be along the corridor. You want to eat with me again? I'll pick you up at twelve."

Caution of a lifetime dictated no, thank you, and then she remembered how wrong she had been about Tse's motives for mentioning the fifty dollars he was owed by her

45

cousin. "All right. My turn to pay."

"I don't care. What's your name? Your first name."

"Lucy."

He tasted the word. "Lucy. I'll call you that. You call me Peter. You can't pronounce my last name, anyway. The way you say it, it sounds like somebody else. Peter. Not Pete. Okay?" He flashed his teeth and went back to his own office.

Again Lucy wondered whether a bowl of vegetable soup and the use of her first name added up to a pass in Chinese, and she looked at herself in the huge mirror that stood near the back wall and told herself not to be silly. Just to be thinking in these terms made her feel ridiculous, but she was a long way from Longborough and she didn't want to make a fool of herself or reveal the various kinds of naïveté that she was feeling.

She was interrupted in the process of trying to get comfortable in her situation by a knock on the door. Immediately after the knock, the door opened and a middle-aged man in a short-sleeved shirt and khaki pants entered and sat down. Before she could stop him he had taken an envelope out of his shirt pocket and spread three pictures on the desk, moving aside the bric-a-brac to make room.

"This is the man my wife called about. We want to know where he is, if he's safe." He looked hard at her. "My wife made an appointment with Mr. Trimble. Is he in? You know about this?"

"Mr. Trimble is no longer in business. He's dead. I'm his cousin."

"You his partner?"

"No, the business is closed. I'm just clearing out the office."

"I made an appointment." He stared at her aggressively. Eventually he heard what Lucy had said. He gathered up the pictures. "I'll have to go somewhere else, I guess. Shit."

"Have you lost someone?"

"You could call it that. My son. He's disappeared. Over a week ago. Personally, I'm glad. I've been trying to get him out of the house for ten years. He's thirty-three. But my wife is worried, so I'd like to find him so I can have some peace." He considered what he had said. "He's not *my* son. This is my second wife; he moved in right after we married. He lives in the basement, breeds tropical fish. We came home from a movie last Monday and he was gone. Took his favorite fish with him, thank Christ. I told my wife, if he's taken the fish then he hasn't been kidnapped. Nobody's going to take a tank full of goddamn guppies, are they? No kidnapper, I mean. But she wants to know he's all right."

"I can't help you, I'm afraid. If you want a detective agency, try the Yellow Pages. Maybe you said something to offend him."

"Yeah? I wish I knew what. I'd make a sign and hang it out the front window."

Chapter 6

Lucy wondered how many more like him might appear. It was a long way from her first fantasy about Trimble's world: no distraught, beautiful molls, pleading for help; no man with blood trickling from the corner of his mouth, gasping the two words that meant everything before he died in the doorway; no foreigner with the Luger and the thick accent. She knew why, of course, for none of these characters had appeared even in Lucy's fiction for at least twenty years. As she had known before she inherited her cousin's business, real private detectives deal with shoplifters, not assassins. Searching for a missing tropical-fish fancier was probably typical. And yet . . .

She turned to the computer. Peter Tse had said that this was probably where Trimble stored his recent records, and she set about retrieving them. She had been trained by the library in the elements of WordPerfect, and she had no trouble calling up the files. Trimble had not developed many.

The first was labeled NEWCL, which she

guessed correctly meant new clients. Tse was right about the slowness of Trimble's detective business. In the last six months there appeared to have been four new clients, and none of their cases looked interesting. All except one were what Trimble called "surveillance," watching homes to see who came out and went in over a given period of time. Each ended with a dull little summary, a report, which Trimble presumably printed to give to the client along with his bill. There was no mention of money received, and Lucy suspected that Trimble was not in the habit of keeping accurate records of untraceable income, fees paid in cash. The exception to the surveillance cases was a missing-persons case. Trimble had apparently found the person, a runaway girl, in twenty-four hours by going down to a young people's shelter on Yonge Street.

Watching for adulterers and looking for strays. It didn't seem very difficult. What about someone who had been missing for a year? Or twenty? What if someone was trying to trace a relative, someone who emigrated from Scotland, say, twenty years before, a situation that was close to the center of about a third of the mystery riddles she was familiar with? Where would you start? Lucy found herself musing over whether her library experience would help. The fantasy, the notion that she might try her hand at her cousin's trade had been lurking at the edge of her consciousness from the time that Walter Buncombe had told her what Trimble did for a living.

Lucy was completely aware of the situation she was in. She was a voracious reader — even Geoffrey had not been able to limit that — and she had read not only most of the crime section of the Kingston Public Library, but a fair amount of the mainstream fiction also, including Jane Austen. She was familiar with *Northanger Abbey* and believed herself in no danger of mistaking the real world of her cousin, the "watcher," for the world of the private eye romances she was fond of, not at forty-seven years old.

And yet, now that she had confirmed the truth, she began to wonder again, in a different way. If all that *real* private detectives did was watch, she could surely do that, couldn't she? What about missing persons? What records would exist? In no time at all she was in the middle of a daydream involving lost heirs, changed names, new and assumed identities, all of which Lucy Brenner would unpeel to the core with the help of her library training.

She shook herself and called up the next

file. It was labeled KINGDOM. The first page began,

The black, billowing clouds that had promised to drop their ominous loads from the beginning of the equine proceedings parted momentarily as a shaft of golden sunlight pierced the sky to light up a red cap in the middle of the group of straining horseflesh. The eight superbly conditioned descendants from the teeming loins of those four original Arab stallions swept together round the curving timbers of the final bend to grapple with the last furlong. In the middle, Night Fighter, my favored steed, threaded its red-capped rider through the throng as I cheered myself hoarse. It seemed as if "Paddy" O'Rourke, that wizard of pace from the "ould sod," had worked his magic again because his mount gathered its mighty muscles in the last few yards for a titanic effort, forcing his head under the wire by the inches it needed to be my first winner. Nothing again would ever equal that first thrill, but I have had many like it.

The narrative stopped here, then began again. This time the eight superbly trained descendants of the fertile Arabian imports preceded the black, billowing clouds, and the syntax was adjusted to heighten the drama, each sentence getting its own paragraph. Trimble's labor of love, his life story in the form of a history of his greatest wins, continued with many revisions for seven pages, roughly a race per page. Then it stopped for a series of titles:

My Kingdom for a Winner
A Bet in Time
Days at the Races
Turf Love
Life Among the Longshots
A Mare's Breadth

Then a new narrative began:

The next two minutes would decide his fate. Jack Crabshaw patted the service revolver in his pocket, knowing he had the courage to use it if he had to. Hadn't he almost done so in '59 when his burnoose had slipped on the way to Mecca? His house, his business, his family's well-being, the surgery his crippled daughter needed, all were riding on the six-to-one shot now being loaded into the stalls. He had scraped and borrowed every cent for one last bet, the one that would finish it, one way or the other, forever. "They're off."

A paragraph later, the black, billowing clouds parted once more and Night Fighter again saved the day.

This narrative in turn began again. This time, Night Fighter lost. Jack Crabshaw sought out a quiet place under the stands to shoot himself, but, crouched there, he overheard the owner of Night Fighter explain to a crony that the race had been fixed, that Night Fighter had been held up. Now Crabshaw decided to shoot the owner of the horse.

The file was thirty pages long, moving continuously between fiction and nonfiction as Trimble tried to make literary capital out of his obsession. Toward the end, a new story began:

Chapter One
  "They're at the post."
Jacob Yeo lifted his glasses to watch the starting gate. This was his last chance. His house, his business, the surgery his crippled daughter needed, everything was riding on one last bet, this five-to-one shot he had been train-

ing for this moment. This would finish it one way or the other.

"They're off."

Dome Light was slow out of the gate. Something was wrong. He could make it up, surely, but already he was ten lengths back of the field, his head down, his tongue hanging out. Solar Plexus had raced into an early lead and was now in front by a wide margin. As they approached the last bend, Yeo began to pray. It was now or never. But the gap widened. When Solar Plexus passed the post Dome Light was still twenty lengths behind the rest of the field.

Mechanically Yeo walked to the unsaddling enclosure and went through the motions.

"What happened?"

The jockey shrugged. "He's been got at," he said.

The signs were unmistakable. The yellow foam round his mouth (check this), the heavy sweating — he had been drugged. Out of the corner of his eye, Yeo saw the jockey on Solar Plexus watching them, and he knew then where to start looking. Yeo was ruined, but he wouldn't go quietly. He intended to find out who had done this thing and kill them, one by one, starting with the jockey on Solar Plexus. (This is it. Move to a new file.)

As far as Lucy could tell, the enterprise was hopeless. She recognized in Trimble one of those people that librarians know all about, the army of Sunday writers whose stories had *really happened*. Until now, Trimble's obsession with horses had not interested her; in fact she was dismayed that a grown man could be so consumed, but she could warm to Trimble the writer, for she saw that some of his heroes were among her own, the writers of thrillers about horse racing (although there was something about Trimble's prose and story line that suggested an older generation of tales than those currently on the bestseller lists — Nat Gould, perhaps — in spite of the dozen or so novels of Dick Francis that had been strewn about the floor by the burglars), and her heart went out to him for wanting to emulate his heroes. He was as romantic about the world of horses as she was about his world.

The file ended with a list of phrases, more titles, notes for future anecdotes, and a series of notes in the form of reminders. Lucy went back to the file directory and found W\JUSTICE and called it up. The full title was WILD

JUSTICE and a glance told her it was the same story as the one in the memoirs, but it began farther back in Yeo's life. Trimble had evidently felt that he had found his subject at last. Lucy returned to the list of files, finding one called DIARY and trying to retrieve it, only to be informed by the screen that the file was protected by a code. It was secret. Honor told her to keep it that way even while her curiosity began casting about for the possible code word.

She was interrupted by Peter Tse, come to take her to lunch.

Chapter 7

"What else do you have to do?" Tse asked, when they were drinking tea at the end of the meal.

"This afternoon I'm going to pack up the clothes for the Salvation Army, and see the morgue people for his wallet and things."

"Then you're going home?"

"For the night. I have someone coming in Longborough. I'll be back tomorrow, though. I might stay around for a few days."

"Waffor?"

She was not ready to answer yet, not ready to admit to the small riot of desire that had sprung up in her breast, the "what if" concerning the possibility that if Fate existed, then she (Fate) was providing Lucy with a chance to leave the library behind. Lucy reminded herself yet again that no one knew better than she that there was nothing glamorous or exciting about the world of the private detective, and now the rationalization, honed and polished already, slid smoothly into place: It was surely just that knowledge of the humdrum ordinariness of the private detective's world that allowed her to consider herself perhaps suited to it? She had already seen enough of her cousin's business to guess that it was marginal at best: Perhaps she could make something of it. And along with her desire to take over the business was her awareness that the other seed, the doubt about her cousin's death, was sprouting not far below the soil. And finally, she told herself, becoming a private detective would be a perfect cover to accommodate her real need, the need to move on. David Trimble's business would provide her with the justification, give her a response to all of her Longborough friends who worried about her, and to her daughter, who had to be continually reassured that her mother knew what she was doing.

Thus the process had started, but it was not yet far enough advanced to let her declare herself. "I haven't sorted everything out yet," she said.

"What is there to sort out?"

Impatient, cornered, scrambling for a story, she invented. "David was writing a novel. I thought I would see if there was anything to it."

Tse burst out laughing. "David? A novel?

It would be all about horses. He didn't know anything else."

"It is. Still, I ought to have a good look at it, don't you think?"

"David couldn't write a novel." Tse roared again.

"Why not? By the way, why do you sometimes say 'anyfing' instead of 'anything'? Does Mandarin not have the 'th' sound?"

Tse stopped grinning and didn't answer for several seconds, and Lucy worried that she had delivered, to a Chinese, the greatest possible insult. All she had been trying to do was divert him from the subject of why she was going to stay around.

"I don't speak Mandarin," Tse said. "I don't even understand it. Maybe it's because I grew up in Soho, in London. I never knew I had an accent. Nobody ever mentioned it before."

"It's only sometimes. Just now and then you can hear it. I thought it was interesting, you know the way you have to be born hearing some sounds in order to pronounce them properly. I hope I haven't offended you. We have a girl in the library . . ."

Tse held up a hand to stop her babbling. "I don't care," he said. "Let's go back."

A slim, dark-haired man in his early thirties wearing horn-rimmed glasses was waiting outside the agency door. He looked from Tse to Lucy.

Lucy said, "Can I help you?"

"I was looking for Mr. Trimble."

"He isn't here anymore. I own the agency."

He looked consideringly from her to Tse. "You work here?" he asked.

Tse said, "I'm the landlord."

"What happened to Mr. Trimble?"

"He died," Lucy said. "What can I do for you?"

"You mean you're taking over?"

It was clear that these questions were not seeking urgent answers; they were simply creating a holding action while the man considered the unexpected situation.

Lucy said, "That's right. Can I do anything for you?"

Again the man considered her, appraising her rather than the question. He made up his mind, smiling slightly. "Yeah. I think so. I think you'll do fine."

"Come in, then." Lucy cut through a slight "take-charge" air that her landlord was giving off, a look of wanting to protect her. "Thank you, Peter. See you later." She ushered the stranger in and closed the door on a wondering Tse.

61

When they were seated, the stranger explained. "I want you to follow my wife on Thursday nights," he said.

Lucy pretended to consult her diary, recognizing this as the point of no return, the point at which she ought to excuse herself. Instead, she said, "I think you'd better elaborate." That sounded right. "Follow her where?"

"My wife suffers from agoraphobia."

"Fear of heights?"

"That's acrophobia. Agoraphobia is a fear of open spaces. She hasn't been able to leave the apartment for a year, but I think she's improving. At any rate, I've taken her out several times and now I'd like to see if she can manage on her own."

Old-fashioned common sense told her that this man should be shown the door, but there didn't seem to be anything in what he was proposing that should make her feel apprehensive. Surely she could follow an agoraphobic around for an hour or two, without a major decision? Perhaps there would be others. She might specialize. "If she panics, do you want me to bring her home?"

"Don't go near her. Not under any circumstances. She's got to cope on her own. If she panics, she'll come home."

"Why do you want her followed?"

"Just a precaution. I'd like you to tell me where she goes, and how she seems to be able to manage." The stranger crossed one leg over the other and laced his fingers over his knee in a chatty gesture.

"Do you have a picture of her?"

He was ready for this, reaching into his jacket pocket for a picture taken in profile of a woman with near shoulder-length blond hair wearing a green raincoat and a matching rain hat. It was an awkwardly composed picture, seeming to be a snapshot taken without the subject's permission, and taken inside a room.

"How long will she go out for?"

"From eight until she can't take it anymore. Not late, at first."

"Why don't you follow her? No, I see, if she sees you, it won't be a fair trial."

"Right. She's got to feel she's on her own."

"Of course." Lucy swallowed, and turned to the window. She didn't like the look of her first client — he seemed sly — and she was slightly dismayed to realize that this would probably be the case in the future, more often than not. People who hired private detectives, like people who pursued grudges with the help of lawyers, were likely to be misanthropic, suspicious, unlovely, even if, as was the case here, they were prompted by concern for another. She could not imagine any of the agreeable people she knew having someone watched by a detective. She had imagined that she would in some way be helping people who deserved to be helped; she still hoped that would be the case occasionally, but she guessed that most of the people who hired her would be like this man, or worse. After all, the agency was like any other business that dealt with the public; it could not choose to serve only the nice customers. They were in too short supply.

Through the window she saw a bustling Queen Street, a streetscape by a naturalistic painter, Kuralek perhaps, a scene of Chinese greengrocers, dollar stores, cafés, and clothing shops. On the second floors she could read advertisements painted on the windows for a travel agency, a firm of lawyers, and an optician. A block away, the pedestrian crosswalk held up traffic so efficiently that the streetcars and automobiles moved more slowly than the cyclists and not much faster than a briskly walking pedestrian. It wasn't New York or Los Angeles, and Queen Street did not look very mean. In fact it reminded her of a sentimental Hollywood depiction of New York's Lower East Side in 1910, but a lot more alive and interesting than the view from the basement window of the Longborough library.

"All right," she said.

"Will you do it yourself?"

All my other operatives are busy, Lucy wanted to say, as she recovered her humor. "I'll do it myself, yes."

"How much do you charge?"

"Fifty dollars an hour, minimum four hours," she replied. She had been working on remembering Trimble's hourly rate for several minutes. "Plus expenses." The man looked prosperous enough.

It would be a relief if he said no, anyway.

"What expenses will there be?"

"If she goes to a restaurant I'll have to buy a meal to keep her under surveillance. And there's movie tickets. Eight dollars except on Tuesdays. The first two hundred is payable in advance."

"I thought it might be. I doubt she'll go to a movie, not at first." The stranger took out his wallet and counted out ten twenties.

Lucy saw that most of Trimble's income was probably tax free. She dropped the money into a drawer, the way she had seen it done in movies.

"I'll give you an accounting weekly, with my report."

"Why don't I just come in each week and you can tell me where she was and what she did?"

"If that's what you want."

"That's what we'll do, then. Now, here are the details . . ."

Before he left he agreed to telephone her the next day to confirm that he wanted to go ahead. "We always give clients a chance to change their minds," Lucy said, hoping Tse wasn't in the corridor, listening. "If you do, you'll get the money back. Now you'd better give me your name."

"Lindberg," he said. "James Lindberg."

She made a note on the cover of a file folder. "Right, Mr. Lindberg. We'll look after you."

She was over her dismay now, and left breathless by the success of her impersonation, and perspiring, still wondering when she ought to stop. As a student of the genre, she had had no trouble with the initial interview. The scene formed the first chapter of dozens of the books she had read. It was in the next chapter that anything could happen, even though Chapter One was bland enough, and when the stranger phoned tomorrow she should tell him to get another detective. She was too busy. Another little anecdote to entertain

The Trog and the librarians.

But she knew quite well that her interview with Mr. Lindberg was no impersonation; it was her first day in her new job.

Chapter 8

Back in Trimble's apartment to dispose of the clothes and furniture, Lucy was saddened by the paucity of her cousin's worldly goods. A couple of cartons of clothes would go to the janitor, a Salvation Army truck would call, and David would disappear. As far as she knew, there hadn't even been an obituary notice in the paper. She recalled her silly lie of finishing the novel on the computer, and knew that Tse was right. What she had seen could not be turned into anything publishable.

And then she had an impulse, born of the memoir on the computer and of the bits of writing she had done in Longborough, an impulse to commemorate David in some way, to write a little account of his life and what he meant to his friends so that he would not disappear without a trace, like Willy Loman. There was an article there, surely. The *Examiner* might run it, or one of the racing papers. A little essay. She thought about titles. "The Last Race," she thought; then, more irreverently, "Death of a Bad

Bugger." She would talk to all his cronies. Surely a man's life was worth a thousand words? And as the scheme came to her, she knew that she had found the answer, the perfect excuse that would let her do what she wanted to do, which was to stay here, and see what happened next.

She postponed telling The Trog until after dinner. She was coming to a decision that she felt everyone, including The Trog, would try to talk her out of because he would no longer be able to count on her being alone in Longborough when he came off a mission.

The presence of The Trog in her life had been Lucy's first proof to herself that she had earned the right to a larger existence than Geoffrey had allowed her. The Trog had arrived one night on her doorstep in the early days of her bed-and-breakfast venture, looking for a room. His name, he said, was Ben Tranter. He was in his early fifties, shortish, bald, brown-headed, with a lot of white teeth set in a broad, short face divided by a large, sharp-edged nose. His car had broken down on Highway 28, and the garage had suggested Lucy's establishment as a good place to stay overnight while they fixed the engine. He asked for dinner, which she advertised that she would provide on request. Usually she required a few hours notice in case she didn't feel like offering it, but there was a raffishness about her visitor, a carefree air as if he were descended from a race of tinkers or gypsies, that intrigued her, made her want to take chances, and he clearly seemed to want to find himself at home here. While he was in the shower, she slipped out and bought a chicken pot pie and some tabouli salad (he looked slightly Middle Eastern) from The Movable Feast, a take-out shop where the cooking was a lot more interesting than hers, and had her instincts about him confirmed when he produced two bottles of wine to drink with the meal.

Afterward, the last of the wine drunk in front of a little log fire, he asked for her.

It was the first time anyone had propositioned her for fifteen years, and even then it had been only the occasional colleague of Geoffrey's. The whole situation being presented now was so close to that of the traveling salesman and the farmer's daughter that she immediately rejected the idea as absurd. She laughed and sipped her wine, and thus allowed the second thoughts to come. For although she was out of practice at even the most rudimentary flirting, and although Tranter was not the sort of man she was familiar with, she had known he was going to ask and she had made no attempt to keep her distance.

Setting aside the farmer's daughter, she felt also that their situation was very similar to one that a Longborough friend had confessed had happened to her in Oslo when she had been on a tour of Scandinavia; she had been propositioned by a shopkeeper who contrived to find out her hotel and room on the pretext of promising to deliver a catalog of his leather goods. "I decided then and there that if he asked me I would, because no one could possibly know about it. I've never heard of anyone from Longborough going to Oslo for a visit. So he did and I did, and I had a great time, knowing I would never see him again. I've never regretted doing it with my Norwegian. I expect he has two or three Canadian ladies a week in the high season, but that's all right with me."

And then, between sips of wine, Lucy was reminded of something that had happened to her the year after high school, the only time she had ever been in love, and she had said no and he went away to college and she had never seen him again, and she had regretted saying no ever since.

So now, as she became aware that she was

about to be propositioned, she found herself, without having suddenly fallen in love or become weakened by desire, wanting to say yes rather than no. She needed to prove to herself that she was free to say either, and the only way to be sure of that was to say yes. She was also curious. Geoffrey was her only experience so far, and in these circumstances she felt like a virgin. It was possible that it would be completely different with someone else.

She was vindicated by feeling no regrets whatever. Her husband had always preferred not to see what he was doing, but Ben left the lights on and made himself at home in bed, giving the lie to Circe's legend by being completely unvulnerable in his nakedness. Lucy found the experience exhilarating.

He disappeared in the morning before she was awake (although breakfast was included), leaving the rent on the kitchen table, and she did not expect to see him again. (If she had thought he might return, she would probably have said no that first night.) He had been a manifestation, a sign, arriving at exactly the right moment when her new freedom needed a test. Saying yes was a risk, but saying no would have been a defeat. He had done his job, then; there was no need for him to appear again. But when he returned a month later after calling a day ahead, she put up a NO VACANCY sign on the morning of his arrival. This time he came with champagne and lingonberries and reassured her that on that first night nothing was farther from his mind until after he met her. Again he left in the morning before she was awake, and now she was embarked on an affair.

A dozen times in the next six months he came back, and in the course of that time shifted from the fabulous to the real. The first story he told her about himself was almost certainly untrue, but instinct told her not to press him. At some point, she was sure, he would fade into the light of common day, but in the meantime she hugged the idea of him to herself as the secret that distinguished her from what the world saw, as evidence that she was not a part-time librarian by nature. "The Trog," she named him, a creature from another world, her huge secret that sometimes, when she was with her ladies book group, made her slightly giddy, wondering what they would say if she announced, in the middle of a discussion of the believability of a relationship some novelist was portraying, that she had a lover, too. "Our relationship is entirely sexual," she would say.

"But we like each other, of course." Occasionally she woke up during a dream that she had been discovered, that she had failed to pull the blinds quite closed, that fire was sweeping through the house making it necessary for her and a naked, bald, brown-headed lover to leap for safety into their neighbors' arms. It was a nightmare even in these times, for Longborough was too small not to notice what its librarians were up to.

He was a mining engineer, he told her, separated from his wife, who refused to divorce him. During his early visits he told her about his travels. On his first visit he had been looking for bauxite formations in northern Quebec. The survey party had flown back to Montreal after two weeks in the bush, and he had detoured to Longborough on his way back to Toronto to let off a couple of hitchhikers, two German teenagers he had picked up outside Kingston.

The second time was planned. Having found Lucy, he came to her as soon as he landed from an assignment in North Africa, where he had been looking for oil. The later stories followed the same pattern — he had been in northern Scandinavia, or Australia, or Venezuela, where his company had been prospecting for silver or uranium or gold, and his first destination, once he was free, was Longborough.

Lucy was naïve and intensely romantic, but she was not a fool, and it was obvious to her early that Ben's accounts of his travels were pure invention. His stories were full of holes (what was he doing just arrived from Greenland with a three-day-old *Globe and Mail* in his car?), but he put up a wall against the lightest questioning, seeming to admit even as he denied it that he was a man whose mission was not his to share, sticking to the patchwork of lies that developed ever more holes as she compared the stories he told on different visits. Somehow he contrived to project a curious integrity under the lies. Caught out in a contradiction, he simply backtracked until he found some kind of explanation. If, as occasionally happened, Lucy immediately pointed out to him the incongruities in the new story, he made adjustments until the story worked. It was as if he was saying, "We both know I'm lying. One day I'll say why, tell you the truth, but right now I can't share it with you."

When she had time to think about it, Lucy was not put off by the fact that her lover was a liar. The point was that he was a lover, not a potential husband or mate of any kind, and knowing he was a liar enabled her to enjoy the connection, and profit by it emotionally, without having to worry about the future. There could be no future with such an unknown quantity, but he was very good for her in the present. There was no hint of the sinister in him.

By the time the truth came out, Lucy was more than halfw~y toward guessing. The key to it was that he lied to her like an adult deflecting a child's curiosity away from areas the child wouldn't understand, like sex and death. She was sure that The Trog's mystery had nothing to do with a wife, or another woman, the obvious reasons; he had never hinted at either, though she gave him plenty of openings. No, what he really was or did was either illegal or dangerous.

Then one day he arrived late at night and asked if he could stay for a couple of days. He needed to be out of sight, he told her, and now, finally, she learned the truth. Ben, it turned out was an intelligence agent, a spy. Each time he visited her he had just returned from a mission (in the same place he had said before that he had been prospecting), and as soon as he was debriefed, he headed for Lucy. The story about northern Quebec and the hitchhikers was true, but he had gone up there on the trail of a terrorist who was hiding out in Canada after a failed as-

76

sassination attempt in South Africa.

For someone of Lucy's literary tastes, it was the only thing that made sense of him (although the three-day-old *Globe* was still a puzzle). The day he told her he had blown his cover and needed somewhere to hide, she took his keys and parked his car out of sight behind the library and watched the street for two days while Ben made phone calls. On the third day Ben pronounced himself in the clear — his opponents had been identified and picked up by his own side, he said — and he drove off.

Chapter 9

He came back two weeks later with two bottles of white Burgundy and a stone jar of Gentleman's Relish, which he said he had picked up in Harrods on his way through London.

Her belief in Ben, the secret service agent, lasted for about a month, then gradually she began to know that this story, too, was as fabricated as the story of the mining engineer. There was something about the openness with which Ben discussed his missions when he came to her after each one. In her novels, the women had never known anything that they could betray the hero with, and even though she was unlikely to meet Ben's enemies, he told her far too much. And the three-day-old *Globe* insisted on an explanation. From this and other signs, she knew he was still lying — how had he put two thousand kilometers on his car in the week he was supposed to be in Prague? — but decided not to do anything about it. Although she was intrigued to know the truth, she was afraid now that it would turn out to be fairly humdrum, involving a wife after all, and perhaps a job that embarrassed him, rodent extermination perhaps, and if she pressed him he would simply go away, and she enjoyed his visits too much to want that. On the human level, the level that worried about murderers, she trusted her instincts and felt utterly safe with him. Occasionally she wondered if the truth wasn't that Ben was having the first major experience of his mature years, too, but his ease in bed suggested otherwise.

They never discussed what for want of a better word she thought of as their relationship, and much of her pleasure lay in the way he assumed that this sort of thing was as natural to her as it was to him. After six months, it was. Lucy discovered that you could assume a vice as well as a virtue and pretty soon grow into it. Occasionally she contemplated how she would explain Ben to Geoffrey, and thus remained sharply aware of the distance she had traveled with Ben. For Geoffrey was still around. After a year, "the experiment," as he called it to their acquaintances in Kingston, was still going on. He telephoned, and even appeared occasionally, staying long enough to fix a broken step or a tap washer (but never overnight), and always asking her when she was coming home. It would be as easy to tell him about Ben as to admit she had joined a coven.

And yet now, after two years in Longborough, her life, even though it included having The Great Impostor for a lover, was beginning again to leave her unfulfilled. There was more to come, she felt sure, and although she was too modest to put it into clear words, her successful adventure with Ben was surely proof that she was ready to move on from Longborough when she got the chance.

Now, back in Longborough for the night, she was listening to one of Ben's most elaborate tales, the story of his last job. "He was a guy I'd seen once in Helsinki. No one else had ever seen him, but they knew he was in the States and they tracked him to upper New York State."

"How did they do that if they didn't know what he looked like?"

"The computer boys got a fix on him. They analyzed his patterns, and then they sent me down the hole to ferret him out. It took me a week."

As usual, she had no difficulty pretending

to believe him. "You do look a bit tired. Have some more whiskey." There was no need to challenge him yet, or perhaps ever.

The Movable Feast had outdone itself. *Tourtière* with chili sauce, tabouli salad, and butter tarts. As usual, Ben had brought the wine, a bottle of Australian Burgundy, and a bottle of Macallan malt whisky that he said he had picked up at Charles de Gaulle airport and claimed was the best in the world. They were drinking in the second-floor sitting room where they could not be seen from the street. Summer was the awkward time for entertaining Ben. Now they were slightly drunk and soon they would go to bed, and it would have been nice to sit out in the garden first, but she wouldn't risk it, believing that anyone passing in the street would be able to tell the way they were, as she could spot adulterers at a party.

She stood up and put her glass on the mantelpiece. Tentatively, she said, "I may be moving, at least during the week. To Toronto."

"Why? You got a job there?"

"Sort of."

"Will you have a phone? And a place I can come to?"

"I'll find somewhere without any neighbors."

"Good." Ben stayed where he was for a few seconds, then hauled himself out of his chair, sliding his hand over her bottom as he rose, making her jump slightly. "In the meantime . . ." he said.

Afterward, in bed, when she was straightening the duvet and shaking out the pillows again, she told him the whole story.

He said, "When did you say your cousin died?"

She told him.

He looked at his watch to check the date and nodded, saying, apparently to himself, "I've been away for a few days."

"You wouldn't have heard, anyway. He wasn't famous."

He sat up and arranged the duvet over his legs. "How do you plan to find out about him, did you say? From his friends? Who are they? Where do they hang out?"

"I'm not sure. Wherever betting people go."

"And you'll be staying in Toronto while you write this article?"

"I'm staying for good. I'm going to keep the agency open, too."

"You won't get any customers."

"I've already got one." She described the assignment offered by James Lindberg.

"Do you know what you're getting into?"

"I can get out of it if I don't like it."

"You're just a girl who can't say no, aren't you? How will I let you know I'm coming?"

"Phone the agency?"

He grunted and slid down under the duvet. "I've got a big job coming up," he said. "I may be away for a long time. I'll tell you what. I should know in a couple of days, then I'll call you. I may have to go away for a few months. Don't worry if you don't hear for a while. I'll be back when it's over. But I'll call before I go."

This time he paid for his room in American dollars.

Chapter 10

"Peter," she said the next morning, using Tse's first name at his insistence, "I'm keeping the agency open."

Tse was trying to make the carpet lie flat under her door. "Be nice if you did stay," he said. "But you don't know anything about detecting." He spoke casually, dismissively, as if to an irritating child, stamping down the edge of the carpet.

"I can learn. I'm going to start by shadowing Mrs. Lindberg, and work up from there. I won't accept anything dangerous. Besides, I want to find out something about David, and I can do it best from here. Do you know any of his friends, his acquaintances?"

"I saw a few of them. Bad guys, Lucy."

"Everybody is, according to you."

"You wouldn't like these people. Bums, deadbeats — one guy who used to bet with David didn't even wash. You always knew he'd been here." He grinned.

"Sounds like Longborough library. Where can I find these people?"

"All at the racetrack. But I am telling you, go back to Longborough."

"You want another month's rent?"

"I don't know if I want to rent to you. I don't like this. You can't follow people about, like David did."

"I'm going to try. At least I've got a car." She moved over to the window overlooking Queen Street. "Who was it that first saw David?"

Tse joined her at the window. "Across there."

"Which one?"

"Nina in the travel agency."

"Nina?"

"She works in the agency."

Lucy crouched down until she got the sight lines right. "How could she see in?"

"The light was on. She looked over and saw David on the floor."

"Then what?"

"She ran over to get someone to break the door open, then she saw me coming along the street. She knows me." He looked across the street at the woman sitting at her desk. "She's my tenant."

"You own that building, too?"

"And the one next to it." Tse switched from his regular Cockney accent to a parody of Charlie Chan. "Chinese man work velly hard, make pisspot full of money while white man watch. Now richest man in Toronto."

"Don't be silly, Peter, and don't swear. What happened next?"

"You married, Lucy?"

"Yes, but I don't live with my husband. What happened next?"

"You got a boyfriend?"

"That's enough. What happened next?"

"I came to the office right away, and there he was, dead. I called the cops."

"You didn't touch anything?"

"I switched off the light and pulled the curtains so no one could see. All the windows across the street were full of people looking."

"Where was he lying?"

"Right here." Tse pointed to the floor by the desk. "I'll show you." He lay down beside the desk. "See?"

"Was there any blood? Were his clothes torn?"

"He fell down dead. A heart attack. He just came to work. He had a cup of coffee on his desk."

"All right. Now I have to see the police."

"Lucy, David was your cousin, right? Why is it you haven't seen him for twenty years?"

"The two families lost touch, I guess. You know?"

"No. My family get together. We like each other. How come Anglo families don't like each other?"

She turned to look at him and saw that he was teasing her. "We do, really. It's just that we don't like anybody much. Now leave me alone. I have to get ready for the police."

Her first stop was the morgue to pick up her cousin's personal effects. She asked the attendant to get rid of David's clothes, taking with her only the envelope of valuables — a billfold with seventeen dollars and two credit cards, a plastic wallet-sized "lens" for reading the small print in telephone books, a watch, a pair of horn-rimmed bifocals.

From the morgue she went to the police headquarters on College Street, where she tracked down the sergeant who had investigated Trimble's death. He listened to her questions, tapped at a computer, found what he wanted, and read it to her:

"David Trimble died of natural causes. A massive coronary. There was an autopsy. No sign of foul play. Take a look."

Lucy leaned over to read the screen. "There was an abrasion on his cheek," she pointed out.

"I did notice that at the time," the ser-

87

geant said. He pressed a key. "Read my report."

The abrasion was noted. It was consistent, the sergeant's report said, with having hit his head on the desk as he fell.

Lucy opened her mouth to speak.

"Read on."

Next came the laboratory report. The technicians had found a trace of David's skin on the metal edge of the desk.

"I see." She thought about it. "Could he have been threatened, frightened by someone who knew he had a bad heart? I know of several cases like that."

"In Toronto?"

"Not in Toronto, no." One was on the Balkan Express in 1936; two others were in England, one in a vicarage, the other at the University of Oxbridge. "But if someone *did* that, wouldn't it constitute a kind of assault?"

"There was no evidence of anyone else in the room, except the landlord who found him. The room was locked. No break-ins, nothing disturbed. It was natural causes, Mrs. Brenner. He was practically an invalid, according to the pathologist. Anything could have brought it on, or nothing."

"But what about this break-in?"

This was news to the sergeant. Lucy told

him what had been happening.

The sergeant listened, then explained. "Queen and Egerton is kind of cosmopolitan. When the word got out that your cousin had died, there'd be any number of local citizens who might decide they'd take a look, pick up anything that's loose."

"But they didn't steal anything."

"Maybe they were looking for money."

"Quite a coincidence."

"It isn't a coincidence, is it? A coincidence has to be surprising. Talk to the Break-and-Enter squad. They'll tell you that there were a hundred and eighteen break-ins in the Queen and Bathurst area last year."

"How do you know?"

"I don't. I'm making it all up. But that would be about average."

"Won't they investigate further?"

"Investigate what? They'll be around to find out if anyone saw anything. But you don't know if anything was stolen. What's to investigate?"

Lucy said, "Did you take pictures?"

"Of the body? You want to see?" The sergeant opened a file drawer and pulled out an envelope. Inside were a dozen color photographs, taken with a flash camera. As Lucy reached out a hand, the sergeant pulled the pictures out of reach. "Hold on. He didn't look very peaceful, and there's . . . other things. Do you know what happens when someone dies?"

It was a detail omitted from all but the most naturalistic stories, but she knew what the sergeant was talking about. "I'd still like to see them."

The major indignity was clear, and Lucy tried to concentrate on David's face and the general position of his body. He did not look in pain, but one eye was open, and his face was dark. Lucy turned the pictures over, one by one.

"What are you looking for?"

"I don't know," she confessed.

"If you find anything, let the forensic boys know. They couldn't."

He had succeeded in making Lucy feel naïve, but she felt a friendliness in him that encouraged her to ask for his help. "There's something else I want to do." She took some breath, nervous of her next idea. "I'm going to write a memoir about him, but to do that I have to speak to his friends. David was writing his own memoirs and there's a lot about different people on his computer, but I don't know who they are." It had struck Lucy that she would perhaps get more co-operation if she implied that material, perhaps of a scandalous nature, already existed on David's computer.

The sergeant waited politely.

"He was a gambler," Lucy said.

"I figured."

"Can you tell me who his associates might be?"

"I just knew him dead. I don't work the gambling scene."

"Could I find someone who could help me?"

"You plan to talk to bookies? Stuff like that? Do you know any names?"

"There are some."

The sergeant looked up a number and punched some buttons on the telephone. "Richard," he said, when he was connected. "I have a lady in my office, relative of David Trimble, guy who died, private investigator. You knew him? You know who he hung around with? This lady would like to know where she could find some of them. Yeah, I bet you would, but would you talk to her? This afternoon. Right." He put the phone down and turned back to Lucy. "He's on the fourth floor. He's busy now, but if you come back late this afternoon, he'll see you."

Chapter 11

Lucy went back to the office and collected all the pictures in which Trimble had been photographed with other people, putting these in a plastic bag. Next she switched on the computer and retrieved the file for MY KINGDOM FOR A WINNER.

Three times the black clouds billowed over the racecourse as Night Fighter came round the bend, but eventually, working her way through the narratives, she came to the material she had noticed the first time, the outline for the future:

1. My First Big Win — Night Fighter.
2. Beating the Odds — How I tracked down J. Cull at the Queen's Plate.
3. The greatest coup of my life.
4. Dual Forecast, both bad. I am told the worst re heart.

The list ran to twenty-three items, most of them apparently accounts of bets Trimble had won. The items were in chronological order and the last three probably occurred in the last year:

21. Beating the odds — How I became Oscar T's least favorite client.
22. Nick of Time — the bet that saved my life.
23. He who laughs last — How I won a bet by coming last.

Lucy read it through and noted names on a slip of paper, folding the note in her purse. Before she switched off, she tried an idea on the DIARY file, which she had not yet unlocked. Perhaps her cousin had simply used his own name to protect the file? But the answer came back with the same result, "Enter Password." She did not think the word would be arbitrary; it had to be significant so that Trimble would not forget it. She would find it when she knew her cousin better.

Peter Tse appeared, and Lucy told him about the locked diary and asked him if he had any suggestions. "Try 'Journal,' " he said. She punched in "Journal." No good. "Try 'Secret.' " No good. " 'Private,' " Tse said. No good. She switched off and Tse asked why she was so keen to get into the diary file. She told him.

"You going to ask the police about his pals?"

"I already have. I'm going back this afternoon."

"Good luck."

She drove first to Trimble's apartment and went through all of his clothes carefully, but her cousin had apparently been scrupulous about his wardrobe, always emptying everything from his pockets before he hung up his clothes. She shook out his shirts and unrolled his socks, but there was not even a stray coin.

Next she emptied the fridge: frozen dinners in sealed packets, canned food, half a loaf of bread. Dumping the bread, she put the frozen food back into the freezer compartment, and the cans back into the cupboard where they belonged.

She was left with the bed, an armchair, a rug, a television set, and a lot of framed pictures of Trimble, all group photographs in which Trimble and one or more other men were posed at the racetrack. The one peculiarity of the pictures was that in each, Trimble was wearing an empty camera case, from which Lucy deduced that all of them were taken at his request with his own camera.

There was nowhere else. The bathroom contained all the expected items as well as

94

a lot of old-fashioned toiletries, including a tin of brilliantine and another bottle of toilet water from Trumper of London. Lucy squeezed, shook, held up to the light, unscrewed, and generally made sure that nothing as big as a nutmeg could have been concealed (she also looked in the toilet tank), and came to the conclusion that there were no secrets in the apartment.

On the way out of the building she bumped into the janitor and asked him what the situation was with David's rent.

"He paid the first and last month, so if you give notice then there is five weeks left."

"Is there a big waiting list for these apartments?"

"Not now. Last year we had calls every day, but lately it's calmed down."

"If I wanted it, could I just take it over?"

"I'll ask the manager. You'll have to sign another lease."

"Would you do that? Ask him for me? By the way, you can have all the clothes in the closet. Throw the underwear and socks away."

"Can I have the shirts? Thanks. Mr. Trimble had some nice shirts. I'll use the socks for rags."

"Take it all. I'll call you in a few days about the vacancy."

"There won't be no problem." He winked and grinned, and Lucy realized she had been bribing him.

When she returned to the office she now thought of as hers, she called Buncombe, the lawyer, and explained what she planned to do. Buncombe was as bad as Tse, pointing out to her, by implication, that she was a foolish, middle-aged woman, far too naïve even to think of getting involved in the boredom, the sleaze, the hand-to-mouth existence of a private investigator. So concerned was he that he dropped his affectations and spoke normally.

"What about the risk?" she asked.

"Forget about the risk. Think about the sleaze. You'll be one step up from a debt collector, about on a par with a magazine subscription salesman."

"I'm going to try it. If it's too sleazy, whatever that means, I'll quit. It won't get boring for a while, at least, and I'm not broke. I can manage. But I may have to pass a test or something. Do you know? Or do you know anyone who knows? You must use private investigators sometimes. For the sleazy stuff."

"Touché. Be it on your own head, then. Go and see a guy called Jack Brighton. I'll call him that you're coming. Then go back to Longborough." He gave her Brighton's address and phone number.

Chapter 12

Brighton's agency, J.B. Investigations, occupied the second floor of a building on St. Clair Avenue, just west of Bathurst, in an office as featureless as Trimble's. Lucy watched the numbers carefully, and when she decided she was close enough, parked in the Loblaw's lot, just east of Bathurst, planning to shop for a few groceries when she was finished with Brighton.

The private investigator was about thirty-five. There was nothing about him to indicate his trade: He might have been a real estate salesman, or a professor of sociology, or even a librarian.

"Sorry about your cousin," he said. "I met him a couple of times."

"How do you know about him?"

"Buncombe called me. To ask me to help you if you came by. So what can I do?"

Lucy said, "I want to take over the agency. Keep it going."

"Why?"

"I'm ready for a change."

Brighton nodded. "So you want me to tell

you how to take away my business? Okay. What do you want to know? You get two licenses from the Ontario Provincial Police, one for the agency, one for you. That's all you need. You won't get much business, though, so why bother? Come and work for me. I'll teach you."

"Why should I work for you?"

"Because I've got two totally boring jobs on right now that you could do. I need some help, and you won't get any work on your own."

"Why won't I? And if so, why would you hire me?"

"Same reason for both. You're a nice, respectable middle-aged lady in from Longborough to do a little shopping. People looking for an investigator want someone lean and mean-looking, like me. But *I* need someone who looks like you, like a collector for the Heart Fund."

Thank God for The Trog, Lucy thought. Without him, that's what I am. "I already have a case." She told him about her first client.

Brighton stopped acting laid-back and listened carefully. At the end, he said, "Does he want pictures?"

"Photographs? He didn't say anything about that. What on earth would he want pictures for? Pictures of what?"

"They usually like pictures to show you've been on the job. Agoraphobia. That's a new one. Who is this guy?"

"I don't know. My client."

"He sounds like a flake. Watch it. She may not be his wife."

Lucy felt at sea. "Then why is he paying me to watch her?"

"She probably knows him, and would run if she saw him. Sounds a little kinky."

"What shall I do?"

"Take the money. Tell him where she goes, but find out who she is. At some point you may have to do something."

"Like what?"

"Like telling her she's being watched. And on whose orders."

Lucy looked at Brighton closely. "You're making this up. Trying to impress me."

He laughed, and blushed slightly. "All right, but it does seem a little weird, doesn't it? If it is his wife, he probably suspects she's up to something on her night off."

"That would fit. What shall I do?"

"Find out a little about agoraphobia, is my advice. Check that they live together. And stay in touch. Let me know how it's going. But find out about her."

"How?"

"*You're* the gumshoe."

"There was another man," Lucy began. Then, "Do you often have to trace missing persons?"

"Sometimes. I just finished one. Found him in thirty-six hours. I just sat in a bar, a drug dealers' hangout, and he walked in the second night, just before they did for me."

"I beg your pardon?"

"They knew what I was, and they knew I wasn't a regular cop, so a couple of guys with braided hair told me to move on. They wouldn't have told me twice. Luckily the kid appeared right after."

When Lucy had understood him, she said, "Looking for people sounds dangerous."

"That's what I'm telling you. Ninety-nine percent of our work is boring as hell, and the other one percent is dangerous. Stay out of it."

"Why do you do it?"

"I love it. I couldn't do anything else."

"Can I ask you one more question?"

"What do I charge? Fifty an hour."

"Thank you." She had that right, then. "May I call you if I need you?"

"Sure. I charge for lessons, though."

Lucy gathered herself together. "I do have one more question. What if you come across a crime being committed, even by your client?" In her reading, this was a standard dilemma that the detectives faced.

"Call the cops. Now, Buncombe said you were from Longborough. That right?"

"Yes. Kingston originally, but Longborough for the last two years. Why?"

"This could be my lucky day." He picked up a piece of paper and spun it across the desk at her. "How about doing this one for me? Get your feet wet."

The paper was a letter from a firm of solicitors in Bournemouth, England, requesting a search as to the whereabouts of Brian Potter, who arrived in Longborough in 1940 at the age of ten to stay with his uncle, a farmer of the same surname.

"He's a relative of someone who died," Brighton said. "That's what those enquiries are about. There may be some kind of legacy, but don't tell that to anyone in Longborough until we're sure we've got the right one. It can't be much, or one of those English lawyers would have treated himself to a trip over here, so there's no hurry. Maybe by the weekend you could take a run up, see what you can find? How about it?"

"You mean it? You want me to do it?"

"You could start at the library." He smiled slightly to indicate that he knew that was where she worked.

Lucy held the letter out to read it again, wondering what to say. She got the feeling from Brighton that he expected her to refuse, that he was making fun of her. "What's the fee?" she asked.

"Twenty an hour, gas and meals. No hotels on this one, and check in every time you rack up six. Don't look at me like I'm a crook. Fifty is what *I* get; I pay you twenty and run the office out of the rest."

"Rack up six what?"

"Hours." He reached for the letter to put it away, giving up on her.

Lucy leaned forward and took the letter from him and put it in her purse, reminding herself she needed a bag to carry things in, maybe a briefcase. "I should have something in a week," she said, naming what sounded like a reasonable period of time, and had the pleasure of seeing that he was slightly nonplussed.

Chapter 13

Sergeant Ibbotson, in charge of the gambling detail, was waiting for her. "Go down to Woodbine," he said. "You know. The racetrack? That's where he spent his time. Why?"

"I want to find out what he was like, what he meant to people."

Ibbotson blinked. "You know what kind of people that might be?"

"Bad people."

"You got it, ma'am. Some of these guys make their living hurting people. You don't want to have anything to do with people like that."

Lucy said, "Just each other, I've heard. They wouldn't hurt me. And my cousin didn't have much to do with the very bad ones, I hear."

"What's it all about, anyway?"

"I'm going to get a license and take over my cousin's agency, and I want to write a memoir about him. My first job is going to be to find out what he was like."

Ibbotson was amused, but he was becoming sympathetic, as if she were an earnest teenager on assignment from her high school newspaper. "What can I tell you?"

"You knew him. Who were his acquaintances?"

"I knew *of* him. He didn't have a record. His friends did, though, some of them."

"Who were they?"

"You want to know who he hung around with?"

"Yes."

Ibbotson shook his head. "I don't think I can talk like this."

Lucy pulled a slip from her purse. "What about these?" She read off the names she had found on the computer in Trimble's memoir.

"Nolan's still around. At least he was when I last looked. He and Trimble were great buddies."

"Where can I find Nolan?"

"Out at the track. Any day."

"What does he look like?"

"We don't give mug shots to the public."

Lucy pulled out the photos she had taken from the walls of Trimble's office. "Any of these?"

Ibbotson glanced at them and shook his head. Then he looked at them again, selected one and said, "Him. Johnny Comstock. He's a trainer, but he wouldn't hang around with your cousin."

"Why?"

Ibbotson looked out the window, saying nothing.

"I see. You mean he's an honest trainer."

"I mean no trainer would hang around with your cousin, and yes, as far as I know, Comstock is strictly on the up-and-up."

"Where will I find him?"

"Same place." Ibbotson looked at the pictures again, then pushed them back to her. "What do you plan to do? Go up to each of these guys and ask him to tell you stories about Trimble?"

"I've got a better idea than that. Thank you very much, Sergeant. May I come back?"

"What for?"

"It's a very new world to me. I might need help to understand what I find out."

"I'll help you right now. Forget it."

"I can't do that. I think my cousin deserves some kind of memorial."

"Peter," she said. "Look at these pictures. I got them off the walls. Have you ever seen any of them before?"

"Him," Tse said immediately, pointing to the picture of Comstock.

"That's where I'll start, then. Tomorrow I'm off to the races."

"Lucy, what are you up to?"

"I told you. I want to write a little memoir about David."

"So you say, but I don't believe you. I've been thinking about you. You think somebody killed David, don't you?"

"No, no, of course not. How could that be?" Lucy moved some objects around the desk like the operator of a shell game.

"That's what you're trying to find out."

"Well, I do think it's strange. I know he had a heart attack, but he might have been threatened, which would bring it on. Why was the office broken into? There's something at the bottom of it. Was there anyone in the office before the person across the street arrived?"

"His door was locked. I opened it."

"Locked-room murders are a dime a dozen. There are books, collections of them."

"It was nine o'clock in the morning. Dave's friends don't get up that early."

But it wasn't good enough. It had to be *proved*.

Tse shook his head. "Well, for God's sake be careful who you ask. I'll come with you to the racetrack."

"That would be nice. I don't even know where the racetrack is. What time do we have to go?"

"The first race is one-thirty. We'll leave at eleven-thirty. Have lunch at the track."

"Good. Now I have to get ready to do my first job."

"What?"

"My first client. I'm keeping the agency. I told you."

"I thought you were kidding."

James Lindberg had said that his wife would be leaving the building at eight o'clock. She was blond, he reminded her, medium height, slim. She parked her car, a dark blue Volkswagen Jetta, license 040 KOO, in a municipal lot on Pleasant Boulevard. All Lucy had to do was wait by the exit, and follow.

Lucy circled the block three times and decided that she could wait just past the garage, near a driveway, so that she could turn quickly if the woman went the other way.

At ten past eight the Jetta emerged, flashing a signal indicating that she would be driving past Lucy on her way out to St. Clair Avenue. Lucy followed closely until her quarry turned onto Mount Pleasant Road, and tucked herself into the slow lane going south. She allowed a car to get between them and settled into pursuit. The woman turned right onto Bloor Street then drove along to Bay and turned north and then west onto Yorkville Avenue, where she left the car in a lot opposite Bellair Street. Lucy followed her in, found a space on the same side of the lot, waited for her to start walking, then quickly trotted after her, trying to keep out of sight.

They walked down Yorkville to a bar near Old York Lane. When her eyes got used to the gloom, Lucy spotted her target in the corner of the room, and she took a seat on the far side, sitting herself so that if the woman tried to leave by the back door, she could follow immediately, aware that it would be easy for the woman to disappear in the corridors around the kitchen and the washrooms. She ordered a gin and tonic, remembering to pay for it immediately so that she could be ready to leave at the first sign from the woman.

They stayed for half an hour, then Lucy followed the woman down Old York Lane to a second-floor restaurant on Cumberland Street. Here Lucy nearly trapped herself, almost bumping into the woman at the top of the stairs where she was waiting for a table in the tiny restaurant. Fortunately she turned away as Lucy appeared, and Lucy stepped back and studied a poster for a few minutes until her quarry was seated by the window, then asked for a table in the back "away from the street." She fiddled with the menu, trying to lip-read the woman's order to the waiter, establishing only that she was having an elaborate meal, then ordered an omelette and a bottle of mineral water for herself. At this point it seemed to her that her heart had been beating at twice its normal rate for about three hours. In the end, she had time to drink two cups of decaffeinated coffee before the woman paid her bill and left.

At this point, Lucy tried to do what she had seen done in the movies a hundred times, to drop a bill on the table and follow the woman downstairs. But she had no idea what an omelette in this place cost, with the two taxes and the tip added in. And the mineral water? And the coffee? She guessed that the total would be about nineteen dollars, so a twenty would not leave enough of a tip. Thirty would have done the trick, a twenty and a ten, but she had only three twenties and some change. Desperate, she dropped two twenties on the table and headed for the door. The waiter barred her way, and she pointed at the money on the table.

"That's too much," he said. "The bill is only fifteen-thirty. Here, let me." He reached past her and picked up a twenty and offered it back to her. "You put *two* down, see? One came out with the other, I guess. Here. You would have missed it tomorrow. Have a nice evening."

This charming, honest waiter had now delayed her long enough to have lost the woman. Then Lucy had a small inspiration and ran to the restaurant's front window overlooking Cumberland Street. The new little park was full of people, and Lucy stared for too long, trying to see the woman among the crowd. Then she looked along Cumberland and there she was, just passing the Bellair Café. Again Lucy was inspired, and instead of tumbling down the stairs to pursue her, she waited a moment and watched the woman turn north onto Bellair toward Yorkville. Before she turned the corner, she looked behind her several times, and now Lucy registered that Mrs. Lindberg had done the same thing on the way to the bar. Lucy wondered if the woman knew her husband better than Lucy did, and was expecting to be followed. Something like a budding professional pride made Lucy want to avoid being spotted by the woman, and when she left the restaurant she took a small chance and turned right, then trotted down Old York Lane into Yorkville, crossing the street immediately to the corner of Hazelton Avenue. When she had tucked herself against the wall and looked down Yorkville, she was pleased to see that the woman was still walking toward her on the other side of the street. Lucy moved off onto Hazelton Avenue to be out of the line of sight, and watched the woman walk past, still checking behind her, then pause, turn, and pretend to read a menu outside Maxwell's Plum. Lucy moved farther into the shadows as the woman now took a long look up and down the street before slowly moving off to the parking lot.

Yorkville was clogged with summer-night cars and strollers, and Lucy felt safe in waiting for the woman to emerge before scuttling in behind to claim her own car. She knew, anyway, where the woman was going, and she followed her, only two cars behind, onto Avenue Road, crossing over to Yonge at Roxborough. It was just ten o'clock. Lucy followed the woman to the entrance of the garage, and waited for her to emerge. Her instructions were to make sure she emerged on foot, then quit. When the woman emerged on foot, Lucy drove home. A hundred dollars plus expenses. Not bad, once she was used to the excitement, but it wouldn't last. The woman was obviously coping quite well or enjoying a minimum amount of freedom, depending on whether her husband was telling the truth or if there was anything to Brighton's suspicions. If Brighton was right, if the woman just wanted a couple of hours on her own, then it was certainly possible she had had a date in the bar who didn't turn up, but at the moment it looked as if her husband had nothing to worry about.

Chapter 14

Tse was dressed in an elegant cream linen jacket, dark gray cotton pants, and a white shirt without a tie. Noting Lucy's surprise when he had appeared to collect her, he said, "My racing clothes. I need pockets. Besides, I've got a date."

"Who?"

"You. You feel lucky?"

"I'm not going to gamble."

"You have to bet. Two dollars to show on an odds-on favorite. You'll win ten cents."

"Or lose two dollars."

"I'll *lend* you two dollars."

"No, I'm not going to bet."

"Then we won't stay. I'm not being at the races with someone who doesn't bet. You'll talk all the time, I'll *give* you two dollars."

"I have my own money. All right, if I have to. How much do I need?"

"Twenty dollars. Two dollars a race if you lose every race."

"I won't know what to bet on."

"Yes, you will. All the nice names. That's what women bet on."

"What are *you* betting on?" Lucy asked.

"The winners."

"Which are they?" She tried to read the list of runners on the race card.

"I'll tell you after I win."

They were sitting in the bar of the club-house, eating hamburgers and drinking beer. Lucy was trying to accustom herself to being continually surprised. In the first place there was hardly anyone here. In fact there were several thousand people, about average for a weekday at the end of the summer meeting, but Woodbine is designed to accommodate thirty thousand. They had parked at leisure in one of the many deserted parking lots and made their way to the clubhouse among a trickle of racegoers, most of them solitary men who looked as if they were on their way to the dentist. Peter took her down to the rail to look at the track, and Lucy had tried to make sense of the huge boards that displayed the odds and wondered aloud where were the shouting bookmakers that she had read about. Tse had explained the differences between racing in England and North America, and they had moved to the paddock to look at the horses. The jockeys were just mounting for the first race, and they waited for them to file past and out onto the track. A horse called Sweet William had caught Lucy's eye, and she found a window and followed Tse's instructions, betting two dollars on him to show.

They seated themselves in the front row of the deserted clubhouse and watched the horses disappear behind the starting gate. In a few moments, eight blurred colored patches with legs started off in the distance. When they appeared round the final turn, they all seemed to be fighting for a single space, but first one, then two, then three horses emerged from the pack and one of them ran past them in front, as Lucy searched the pack, trying to remember her horse's colors. All this time someone was explaining on the loudspeaker how the race was going, doing it with such authority and in such detail that Lucy guessed that the owner of the voice was in the ambulance, keeping pace with the horses on the inside of the track. No one could possibly sort out those colored patches until they came in front of the stands, even with the most powerful binoculars in the world.

"How did you make out?" Tse asked her.

"I never saw mine. I don't think he came out of the gate."

Tse took her ticket from her. "Number six," he said. "Third. You win forty cents."

Watching horse races took practice.

"What did you bet on?"

Tse explained how he liked to behave at the racetrack. "I won't tell you if I win, then you won't know if I lost. At the end I might tell you if I had a good day, but if I didn't I'll say I did, anyway. I don't want you to know if I won, and I don't want to tell you if I lost. It's personal, see?"

"But you know what I bet on."

"Sure, but you don't mind. I do."

"Sorry."

"That's okay. But if you talk about what you are going to back, you talk your luck away. And afterward, like I said, you may not want to admit you lost."

"I'll leave you alone, then. I'm going to find Mr. Comstock. He must be here somewhere. One of his horses is running in the fifth race."

"You need me?" Tse looked anxious. The next race was only ten minutes away. "You won't be able to get into the paddock, anyway."

"I'll just speak to him over the hedge, then."

"Be careful." A routine warning, as to a child.

She made her way downstairs and strolled toward the gate that led into the paddock. A uniformed guard stood by the gate, and

Lucy watched how he dealt with the flow. Here, too, it was quiet, and very few people were going through the gate. Some of those who did wore badges, but others simply nodded to the guard and walked by. Lucy waited her chance, then, when a small group approached the gate, she joined them, matching the last member of the group stride for stride, trying to look rich and bored. Nothing to it.

Inside the paddock she walked over to the most senior-looking official and asked, "Seen Johnny about? Johnny Comstock?" She looked at her watch and up at the sky while she waited for the answer.

"He's with his horse, I should think, ma'am."

Lucy looked around the paddock.

"Back there." The official pointed to a row of horse boxes. "Does he know you?"

Then, before he could question her further, he was interrupted, and Lucy was past.

Chapter 15

Comstock looked too busy to be interrupted. He was talking to a very old lady in a flowered silk dress and white pointed shoes, evidently an owner. Lucy kept her eye on them from a few yards away; when Comstock broke away, she approached him.

He was a comfortable-looking man with the contented look (more common among sailors and horsemen than in most other trades) that comes from having found an excuse to do exactly what pleased him and make a living at it. If any of her favorite novelists had used a character looking like Comstock, Lucy would have set the book aside as a romance. He was about fifty, six feet tall, flat-stomached, with all his own teeth, brown crinkly hair, and a deep tan. He was wearing a tweed jacket, narrow cotton trousers, and ankle boots. He had seen her hovering, and as he waited under the trees for her to come to him, the sun came dazzling through the leaves, making his outline quiver.

When she began to talk, he listened with the air of a man who was not committed to the conversation. As Lucy explained herself further he stepped back into noninvolved territory, signaling with movements of his head that while his body was here, his mind was on the next race.

"I hardly knew your cousin," he said, looking at his watch. "Sorry he died."

"Do you have any anecdotes about him?"

"Nothing you could use. Now I have a horse to see to."

"Can I come and see you when you're not busy?" They were walking briskly along the stable row, Lucy having to skip a little to keep up.

"What about? I didn't know anything about him."

"But you're in one of his pictures."

"So was the Duke of Edinburgh, probably. Look, we kibitzed a little. Just round the track between races."

"Perhaps he mentioned you in his memoirs." This was her ace. She was betting that anyone with something to hide would want to know what was in the memoirs.

Comstock cocked his head as if hearing a faint rumbling sound, and smiled. "Memoirs?"

"He was writing his memoirs, and I'd like to use them to publish something about him."

"There's a manuscript?" Comstock was listening harder now.

"It's all on his computer."

"Trimble had a computer?"

"A word processor. There's a lot of stuff on it, his memoirs, a diary, all sorts of odds and ends."

"A secret writer? Trimble? What's in the diary? Hanky-panky?"

"I don't know, yet. I haven't read it all," she added, realizing, or hoping, that the unlocked diary might also make his friends anxious.

Comstock did not seem anxious, but, rather intrigued. "Okay, let's see. I'm tied up for the next couple of weeks. Some big races coming up. Big for me, that is. What's your schedule? You in the office all the time? Trimble's office? Shall I give you a call?"

"I'm keeping David's office for the moment."

"Same number?"

"Yes."

"You from Toronto?" Comstock looked at his watch, then back at her, this time with some consideration in his glance, as if he had just noticed her. "Look, I'll try and find time in the next couple of days. You can buy me a drink and we can have a chat about your cousin. How's that?"

"When?"

"I'll call you tomorrow."

"All right. But don't put me off then, will you?"

Finally he stopped what he was doing or pretending to do, and laughed. "I was planning to, but I won't. But you know, you ought to be talking to Nolan, Trimble's pal. He'll be the one with the anecdotes."

"That's what someone else said. Is he here? Have you seen him?"

"He'll be here somewhere. If I run into him, I'll tell him you're looking."

Another race had gone by before Lucy found Tse back in his seat.

"Are you winning?" she asked, forgetting his reprimand.

Tse ignored the question. "Did you find him?"

"Yes. Not too helpful, though. He had an old lady with him."

"Yeah?" Tse looked through his race card. "Could be a sign." He studied the *Racing Guide*.

"Are you winning?"

"Shut up a minute." He turned the pages of the newspaper looking for an item he wanted.

"Are you winning?"

"For Christ's sake, Lucy, leave me alone."

"Oscar T," Lucy said.

"What?"

"That was a name on his computer."

"Bloody hell." He slapped his newspapers and race card into a pile. "Look after that." He pressed her shoulder to indicate that she should stay where she was, and climbed down to the front row where a small group of men were arguing. They opened a space to absorb Tse into their group but he pulled out one of the men, a short gray-haired extrovert in a white leather jacket, and spoke to him briefly. The man nodded twice and replied, and Tse returned.

"Oscar Turnbull was a small owner," he told Lucy.

"Where can I find him?"

"He died around Christmastime. Now will you leave me alone?" Tse went back to his *Racing Guide*.

"Nolan," Lucy said.

Tse sighed, looked up, then squinted around the clubhouse. "I don't see him, but he's always here."

"Where can I find him?"

"Here. That's all I know. Sometimes I wonder where the regulars go when there's

123

no racing. It's hard to imagine them any-where else."

"If you see him, would you point him out? He's the last on my list."

"I will. Now, how old was that lady? Old to you?"

"Over eighty."

Tse traced a route over the newspaper with his pen. "That horse has come nowhere in his last three outings. Now they're moving him up a class. Why would they do that?"

"Are you winning?"

"Soon."

They left before the last race.

"Why?" Lucy asked.

"There are guys hanging around watching for the winners. You collect a big payoff from the last race and you'd never make it out of the parking lot alive." He took her protectively by the elbow, glancing nervously around the parking lot.

Lucy watched the racegoers straggle in ones and twos to their cars. There were no hard men that she could see. "I don't believe you."

"Then don't ask."

"You just want to avoid the rush."

"That it? You're a smart one, Lucy." Tse laughed. "How'd you make out?"

Lucy had had five winners: That is, she had backed horses to show in eight races and collected on five of them. She was up about three dollars, but Tse had paid the expenses. "You tell me and I'll tell you."

Tse said, "I held my own."

Lucy understood. "So did I," she said. "I held my own."

Chapter 16

That night, Lucy drove home to Longborough to clean out her mailbox. She had decided not to make any major moves for a few weeks or even months, and thus thought of herself as keeping David's little apartment as a pied-à-terre while she saw how the business went. Weekends she would still spend in Longborough. In fairness to the library, she had told them she would not be coming back immediately, if ever, but she was assured that if she did want to return, they would probably be able to find work for her.

While she was eating her supper of a bacon and tomato sandwich, Geoffrey called. His voice was a shock. "Where were you today?" he enquired, as if he still had the right. "I called twice. Those librarian women told me you had to go to a funeral, and you had stayed in Toronto."

"You know where I was, then." More than anything else she had done in the last two years, more even than her affair with The Trog, her day at the races with Peter Tse and Johnny Comstock had made the world she used to share with Geoffrey very remote. It was as if he was someone she used to know years before. "I stayed over to go to the races," she said.

"You did what?"

"I went to the races."

"Who with?"

"A man I know in Toronto." He wouldn't pursue that, she knew, for fear of discovering that she had found a real alternative to him. She knew how much Geoffrey wanted to go back to the situation of two years ago, knew that she had one last painful piece of surgery to perform to separate them for good. She had been hoping that time would take care of it, that he would realize that their marriage was over, but he showed no signs of admitting it yet.

"Whose funeral was it?" he asked.

Lucy explained.

"Cousin? Cousin? I've never heard of a cousin called Trimble."

"I mustn't have mentioned him, I guess. He was at our wedding. Anyway he's dead and I'm his heir."

"His heir? His heir? What does that mean?"

Lucy's gorge rose steadily as the note of complaint in his voice increased. The man was impossible, but she had suppressed the knowledge by continually intoning to herself his good points, which had finally declined to two: He didn't hit her, and he provided. But freedom had wiped her vision clear, and the idea of coming once more under his nagging, denigrating influence was unthinkable. She explained what the word "heir" meant.

"I know what an heir is! Does that mean you're rich?"

She knew immediately what his concern was. It was not greed, but fear. "Rich" meant "out of my control." Geoffrey was sure that Lucy's little bed-and-breakfast venture would fail and take her money with it, that she would be unable to support herself and that she would then come to her senses and return home, say she was sorry, and he would pull up the drawbridge. All he had to do was wait.

Lucy considered her reply. She had opted for the peaceful way out too often, left him too often still hopeful. Now she said, "The lawyer is just sorting out the estate."

"You *are* rich?"

"I have inherited his business.'

"What sort of business? How much can you sell it for?"

Here, too, she heard at least two kinds of fear. Was the business bigger than his? And did she have some idea of running it?

"It's a detective agency."

There was a silence, then a roar of manu-factured laughter, a mocking, dismissive tor-rent of noise. "Nancy Drew Brenner," he cawed. "Have you bought your magnifying glass yet? You'll need a deerstalker, too." Caw, caw, caw, he went.

She waited until she guessed that he thought he had laid the idea waste, then repeated, "It's a detective agency, and I'm going to run it."

"Very funny, Lucy."

"I'm not joking."

"Now listen to me," he shouted. "Don't be ridiculous. I'm not having my wife mixed up in this kind of thing. Taking pictures of people in motel bedrooms. Some of these people can turn very nasty. You have no experience of them."

"Do you?"

"What?"

"Have any experience of them?"

"Of course I don't, personally, but I know I'm not having my wife play about with them. A lot of low-lifes. And you don't know anything about business. Presumably it *is* a business? Lucy? Are you there? Lucy?"

Lucy was still there. She was resting the phone in her lap as his voice floated up to her. When she heard the interrogative note, she put the phone to her ear. "I won't do anything dangerous," she said, feeling herself slip back slightly into his orbit.

"That's not the point. What am I going to say when people find out that you're sneaking around people's bedrooms, trying to catch adulterers?"

"Those days are over. Detectives don't do that anymore."

"Then what do these so-called detectives do nowadays?"

She chose a phrase from her reading. "Industrial espionage, mostly."

"For God's sake. What do you know about that? Where is this detective business? I'm coming down to Toronto tomorrow."

"No, you're not."

"I'm coming down there first thing in the morning. Where is it?"

What would one of her favorite heroines say? she wondered. The newer, tougher breed. Fuck off? She rolled the words round her tongue. Up your ass, Geoffrey? The thought braced her. "Geoffrey," she said. "I'm not your wife anymore. Stay away. Now and in the future. I'm not coming back to you. Find yourself another lady. I'm getting a divorce. And I'm changing my name back. If you come near me, I'll call the police."

"I'm coming down there tomorrow."

"If you come anywhere near me, I shall get a court order to keep you away."

"You can't do that. You *are* my wife."

"I can try." She took a breath. "Stay away from me if you know what's good for you." She hung up, feeling giddy.

Chapter 17

The next morning, before she went into her office, Lucy poked around the back streets north of Queen, trying to find a place for her car, but the area was jammed. She parked, finally, right on Queen Street, which meant she would have to feed the meter every hour and leave before three-thirty. She promised herself to ask Peter for a better way.

She locked her car and spent a minute trying to decide if it was vulnerable to thieves, but the block seemed busy enough to be fairly safe. She looked up at the building and found she had parked almost underneath her own window, so at least she could look out during the day and check it. Now she looked across the street and noted the window of the travel agency from which had come the first report that her cousin was lying on the floor. The angle seemed strange. The two windows were at the same height, so how could the agent have seen David's body? She crossed Queen Street and entered the building at the door with the agent's sign.

The agency was small, a one-man-and-assistant business it looked like, the office area a bit larger than Trimble's, but part of it partitioned off to give the owner some status. He had apparently not yet arrived. At a desk in the window, an extremely attractive woman of about Lucy's age, with blond hair swept up on top and wearing a red leather suit, was carefully finishing a very crumbly piece of pastry, leaning forward so that the flakes dropped on the paper napkin she had spread on her desk. When Lucy walked in, she leaned right over the napkin, turned her head, and without actually smiling made it clear that she would be smiling in other circumstances. She began the business of getting the rest of the fragments of her pastry from her fingers, her lips, and the surrounding area onto the napkin. Then she folded the napkin, wiped herself off, and deposited the rubbish into a wastebasket. She reached for a Kleenex for the final polish, indicating with her head that Lucy should take the seat beside the desk.

All this took enough time for Lucy to look around the room and realize from the posters that the agency catered to the local Ukrainian population. The telephone rang and the woman answered it, listened, then spoke a sentence in, apparently, Ukrainian,

133

a language that, like Russian, always sounded to Lucy as if it required an entirely differently engineered voice box to create the sounds. The woman put the phone down, smiled at her, then switched voice boxes and said in perfect, musical English, "Forgive me for feeding my face. Can I help you?"

Lucy took a moment to realize that she had been called to order. After her survey of the room she had been admiring the travel agent, her clothes, her hair, her makeup, and her general poise, all of which made Lucy feel a bit of a peasant.

"Oh, yes, sorry. I don't want to travel anywhere. I'm Lucy Brenner."

The agent put out a delicate hand.

"I'm in the office across the street," Lucy said. "The one where the man was found dead. I — er — wanted to ask if I could speak to whoever saw him."

"I'm Nina Sobcyk." The agent looked across at Lucy's office. "It was me. I'm sorry. Was he a friend?"

"My cousin. It's all right. I hadn't seen him for twenty years."

Nina Sobcyk inclined her head politely.

"What time was it?"

"When I saw him?" She thought about it. "Nine o'clock, about. I had only been in about fifteen minutes."

"Who did you tell?"

"It took a little time. I phoned Peter Tse — he is our landlord, too — but he wasn't in yet, so I ran downstairs to get the people in the hardware store or the grocery to go up to his office, but Peter came along the street just then so I told him, and when I came back to the office I could see him in your cousin's office. Then the police and ambulance came."

"How could you see him?"

"He had the blinds open, and the light was on." She looked puzzled by the question.

"No. See. Look. Could I sit in your chair for a moment? Now, look. See? I can't see the floor."

"Of course. I'll show you. Stand up and hold the chair while I get on it. It tilts." She stepped onto the chair, then the desk. "The slat on this blind was stuck and I got up here to straighten it out."

Lucy measured Nina's bottom with her eye. She's as big as me, she thought. I could wear a suit like that. She stood on the chair, waited for it to stop wobbling, then stepped up beside her. Side by side, the two women faced the street a few inches from the glass.

"Where were you exactly?" Lucy asked. "I want to stand in the same place."

"A bit more this way. More yet. Back a bit. There."

Lucy looked across the street at her office. Now she could see David's desk and a portion of the carpet. "You saw him sticking out, of course, from the side."

"I couldn't see his face, but I could tell something had happened to him. I think we'd better get down now." Nina pointed to the street where half a dozen pedestrians had gathered on the curb to watch the two women shuffle back and forth across the window. A fat man in a grocer's apron did a bump-and-grind routine to demonstrate what he hoped they would do next. Nina twisted the slatted blinds closed and the two women got down.

"Did you see anyone in the office?"

"Oh, no." The agent registered mild alarm. "Do you think he was killed? I heard it was an accident, a heart attack."

"I just want to be sure."

"Don't the police think so?"

"Yes, they do. Did you ever see anyone in the office? Would you recognize anyone?"

"This is like *Rear Window*. No. I saw a few people in the six months I've been here, but no one I would recognize." She smiled. "I saw a lot of your cousin. He used to look in the mirror a lot."

"Admiring himself?" Lucy smiled and got up to go. "Thanks for showing me. Can I ask you one more question? Where did you get that suit?"

"This suit?"

"Yes."

"Where did I get it?"

"Where did you buy it?"

"Ackroyd's on Bloor Street."

"Do they have other colors? We're about the same size and it looks terrific on you."

"Yes, but they are very expensive. This was a present."

Dear God, thought Lucy. I *look* like a peasant. Or Geoffrey's wife. "It's very nice. Now I must go to work."

"What do you mean — work?"

"I'm going to take over David's business. David Trimble, my cousin."

The woman looked at her doubtfully.

"I've got my first client," Lucy said, with a touch of aggression. Then, "We can wave to each other from across the street."

Chapter 18

"Peter, give me some more words you might use as secret code words to protect your diary."

They were in her office later that morning, the omnipresent Tse having appeared as soon as she arrived.

"What are you trying to do now?"

She explained.

"His name. Try both names."

She tried "Trimble" again, then "David." No good.

"Maybe he wrote it down, the way people write their social insurance number and bank machine number. Did you look in his wallet?"

Lucy retrieved the wallet from the envelope she had left in the drawer, reminding herself that she had to dispose of his tiepin and cuff links, as well as his glasses. In a secret compartment behind a leather flap, she found one of Trimble's business cards. On the back were the numbers: his social insurance number, his bank account number, and, she guessed, his bank machine access number. There were no words.

"You aren't supposed to keep your bank machine number in the same place as your credit card, are you? You're supposed to memorize it," Lucy said.

"A lot of people write it down, just in case. See, that means David probably wrote the secret word down somewhere."

She took the wallet apart now, hunting for a slip of paper with a word, any word. Together they searched the surface of the desk, among the scraps of paper, the lists, the notes, the telephone numbers, but no likely code word jumped out at them.

"Try 'password.' "

"This is hopeless." She tried it anyway.

"David was a bettor," Tse said. "When you name a horse, you always find a name that is related to its parents. What is 'son of diary'?"

She tried "calendar."

" 'Entry,' " Tse said. " 'Date,' 'month,' 'private,' 'birthday.' "

She tried them all. No good.

Lucy moved on to the next file, titled LEDGER.

Tse hung over her shoulder.

The first entry was "Spittles, 500, Vikings," followed by the date. There followed eight similar entries; each one, two names separated by a number, then the date.

"They are bets," Peter said. "See. Argos. Vikings, Dolphins, Eskimos — they're all football teams. The figure is the bet."

"And the first word?"

"That's the guy who made the bet."

Lucy pointed to one of the names: "Tse." "Do you know him?"

"There's two hundred of us in the telephone book."

"They are very large bets, aren't they?"

"No. Large sums, maybe. Not large bets."

Lucy scrolled the page. "That's a big one," Tse said, pointing to a figure of 1,000.

"What's it all about? Was David really a bookmaker?"

Tse laughed. "He was a drop. People dropped off bets. David passed them on to the bookie."

"You must have seen them. They must have been in and out of the office."

"They used the telephone."

"Did they trust each other?"

Tse laughed. "Oh, no. But they always paid up. The bookies paid up right away, and the customers in the end."

"I see. I think I'd better talk to the bookmaker. He might have all kinds of anecdotes about David."

"You don't know who he is, or where to find him."

"I know who might know."

"You be careful." Tse's response was automatic.

"That's what everyone's saying. I might as well be back with Geoffrey."

Tse left, and Lucy moved to switch off the computer, instinctively saving the file although "the text was not modified." This nudged her into a second instinct, and she searched the desk drawers for a soft disk, found one, copied the ledger, then, as an afterthought, copied the memoir onto the same disk, then put the disk, unlabeled, back in the drawer.

The Trog had not called yet, and this was making her anxious in a way rather different from what she would have felt six months before. She was grateful to him, but she knew now that he had served his purpose. She had decided not to be his occasional lady in Longborough any longer, to move on, and she wanted to tell him so. Since The Trog was her only experience outside marriage so far, she did not know if there was some conventional way of breaking these things off, a way that preserved everyone's self-respect. She was fairly sure it would come as no surprise to him: Lately they had sometimes found little to talk about after he had described his mission, and once he had fallen asleep before she got into bed, and she hadn't woken him up. But she did want to see him for the last time, to tell him it was over. And also, she hoped he was all right.

Geoffrey had not yet turned up, but Lucy knew she hadn't heard the last of him.

Chapter 19

Two days later she drove back to Long-borough to look for Jack Brighton's client, the boy who had come from England in 1940. At this stage, she was keen to show Brighton how reliable she was. If she was going to be able to pay the Toronto rents and keep her house in Longborough, she needed any work that Brighton wanted to farm out.

She started at the library, first picking up a piece of *tourtière* and some salad from The Movable Feast so that she could share the lunch hour with her old colleagues, but she felt somewhat like a college student reluctantly home for the holidays. This was where she used to live, and never would again. Already they were talking about problems, in the library and with each other, that had occurred after she left. She had expected more of a response when she walked in, but while everyone was friendly, they were also working, and she felt slightly out of it all.

The boy's name was Brian Potter and the

uncle had the same name, which meant either that the uncle was the mother's brother-in-law, or that the boy was illegitimate. She found seven Potters in the telephone book, and called them all, one by one, but none of them acknowledged being related to the boy, Brian, in 1940. Next she planned a call on the Bell office to look at the Longborough telephone books from 1940. If that didn't work she would have to make a list of the town's oldest inhabitants and go door-to-door, trying to jog a memory. While she was planning all this, one of the Potters called back to say that his father had just told him that there used to be a family of Potters who owned a farm nearby, and their only daughter had married a man named Denton. She should give them a try. The farm was south of Longborough, near the racetrack. Lucy looked up the Dentons' farm on the municipal rolls and worked out a route.

At one time she could have reached the farm by simply driving south from Longborough, and then east at the right concession road, but a new highway with limited access had been built between the town and the Dentons' farm, destroying the natural crossroads. Lucy got lost on a cloverleaf and ended up at a community college in the southeast corner of the town. A lot of new directions and half an hour later she turned onto a rutted gravel track that led up to some unpainted farm buildings.

As she pulled up, a dog approached her. It was shaped like a very long dachshund, but it was whitish-gray and hairless and it moved as if it were jointed in the middle like a wooden fishing lure. As Lucy opened the car door the animal drew close and slid back its lips, silently, and Lucy pulled her leg in and shut the door. A woman opened the back door of the house and shouted, and the dog wriggled back. "Youse can get out now," the woman shouted to Lucy. "Don't try to touch him, though."

Nothing was farther from Lucy's mind. She stepped carefully past the dog, which so far had simply peeled back its lips to uncover its teeth, without uttering a sound. Lucy called to the woman. "Mrs. Denton?"

"Who wants to know?" Now the woman came forward and passed Lucy to aim a kick at the dog, which was approaching again, but the dog stayed an inch out of range, its teeth still exposed.

Lucy had had time to consider the implications of the rutted farm track, the unpainted buildings, the rusting machinery, the wreckage of a burned car, and the woman's stained dress and broken slippers, and decided that the word "detective" or "lawyer" might have associations that would put this woman on her guard. "I've been asked to find out who lived here fifty years ago," she said.

The woman turned her head and shouted to someone inside the house. "We did," she said, turning back to Lucy.

"Is your name Potter?"

"It was, fifty years ago."

"I'm working for a law firm in England. I'm enquiring after someone named Potter who lived here then. It's something to do with establishing a relationship." Lucy tried to hold her new briefcase open on her knee while she looked for a document.

"You wanna come in?" the woman asked. She leaned back into the doorway. "Henry, we're comin' in," she yelled and waited for a reply, making Lucy wonder what Henry could be doing that required such warning.

In spite of her ancestry, Lucy's only personal experience of rural life was limited to an occasional visit to a farm owned by a lady in her Longborough book club, a farmhouse that glowed and twinkled with the polish that had been applied to the brass and woodwork, and smelled of basil and mint and

146

apples, and heather in the bedrooms. Until now, this, for Lucy, was a farmhouse. The interior of the Dentons' house, the kitchen at least, which was as far as she got, stunned her. First there was the sour smell that hung in the air like an invisible fog, and then the sight of its cause. Henry Denton sat in his undershirt and overalls, drinking beer out of a bottle, watching a bowling match on television.

There was a kitchen table and some chairs. Clothes, a lot of clothes, especially boots, were piled in the corners of the room, spilling toward the center. A sink was full of dishes, and at one end of the counter — Lucy found it hard not to stare at this — a pile of earth and potatoes had been dumped, like a corner of a field brought indoors, to be used as needed.

The woman shouted over the noise of bowling balls knocking against pins, "Turn that goddamn thing off," twisted a chair out from the table for Lucy, then sat down herself.

"You want a glass of water or something?" the woman asked.

Lucy shook her head, wanting most to get out into the air. "As I said, I'm here just to find out what happened to a boy named Brian Potter," she said. "He came here in 1940 from England."

She felt a current of caution run between the Dentons. These were people with a tradition of something to hide, whose response to any question was, first, "Who wants to know?" and "Why?" but, on the other hand, always allowed for the possibility that the stranger asking the questions might not be from an area of government that they routinely lied to, but someone who might just possibly have information to their advantage.

"Who wants to know?" Mrs. Denton asked. "Will you turn that fucking thing down!"

Denton pressed the clicker four or five times, producing a sequence of explosions of color and noise, until he found the "mute" button. "We're in a will," he said to her in the silence that followed, looking sharply back at Lucy, daring her now to deny it.

"That right?" Mrs. Denton asked.

"I'm enquiring about a boy named Brian Potter," Lucy repeated.

"That was my maiden name," Mrs. Denton reminded her. "Potter."

"He was last known to be residing at this address, according to the English lawyers."

There was a long pause while the Dentons considered the implications of any reply they might make. Then Denton nodded to his wife. "He never lived here," she said. "He was sent here to get him away from the war. He was my dad's nephew, so they say. Would have been my cousin."

"So what gives?" Denton asked, sucking thoughtfully on his bottle.

"Would have?" Lucy queried, ignoring him.

Now Mrs. Denton had come to the conclusion that she could safely reveal her next bit of information. "He died," she said. "I'll get the certificate." She disappeared up the stairs.

Chapter 20

The whole visit — the decayed farm, the obscene dog, the squalor of the kitchen — now coalesced for Lucy into a single horror, that there was a ten-year-old boy buried on the farm. She felt as if until now she had been playing about in imitation of her favorite reading, but now she was on the edge of a genre she had never enjoyed, in which detection is quietly mixed with nightmare.

"Here?" she asked.

"He never got here. Story is, her dad went to meet the train he was supposed to be on, and some Red Cross woman told him the kid had died on the train coming from Halifax."

This could be checked. So the only horror was what she had already seen in the kitchen. "You're sure?"

Denton said, "Hey, Missus. Did the kid have any brothers or sisters?"

"I know nothing about that. Do you have any documents to prove his death?"

"Who was it just died, then?" Denton asked.

"His mother, I think."

"Must have been a bit long in the tooth."

Lucy said, "In her eighties, I would think."

"No husband?"

"I think she must have been alone." Lucy thought of a way of giving Denton something to think about. "It could be that she died in poverty and they are looking for someone to pay the bills, the funeral costs."

Denton shook his head. "Everything's free over there. Guy told me. Funerals, stuff like that. The government pays."

"She may have had debts, though."

"Could be." He looked at her, concentrating, his mouth pushed slightly forward in a tight *O*, very much, Lucy could not help noticing, like a protruding anus. "Might have had a few bucks, too," he added.

Mrs. Denton came down the stairs carrying the family papers in a cardboard box. "Be in here, if anywhere," she said.

She hunted through the modest archives, then held up a letter. "Here we are."

It was from a hospital in Quebec, regretting to have to relate the sad news that Brian Potter, aged ten, had died on the trip from Halifax. He had been taken from the train to a rural hospital and died the next day.

Lucy said, "This letter is addressed to the

next of kin. Why do you have it?"

Looking as if she was aware that such questions could be traps, leading to subsequent accusations, Mrs. Denton said, "Because they sent it to us, that's why."

"But why not to his mother?"

"Here," Mrs. Denton said, belligerently, triumphantly. It was another letter from the hospital saying that they had made every effort to find the mother, and they were now forwarding the documents to the nearest relative they could find, in care of a Mrs. Tibbles in Longborough who had agreed to deliver them.

"Where is the rest?" Lucy asked. "There's a list of enclosures, his birth certificate, his English identity card, a picture, his wristwatch, a fountain pen and pencil set, and a wallet."

"They never come." Mrs. Denton removed any suggestion of accusation against her father. "I remember him saying when I asked myself one time. There was nothing else. Just the letter."

"Can I take these?"

"Screw that," Denton said, immediately. "Nora might need those to establish her rights."

"What rights?"

"We don't know yet."

"Then can I copy them, and bring them back?"

Denton considered this. "Copy them out here, you mean?"

"No. I'll use the machine at the library."

"Where's it at?"

She explained in which room the copying machine in the library was located.

"Yeah, but where's the *library* at?"

She told him.

"Right. Near the bus station. That new building. You follow her in," he said to his wife.

Lucy put the papers in her briefcase and clicked it shut.

"Shall I make her a cup of coffee?" Mrs. Denton asked her husband. Denton, in turn, looked at Lucy for an answer, without speaking.

"I'm late already," Lucy said, and walked to the door. "Thanks for the offer."

Denton nodded graciously, and swung himself back to the television set.

Outside, the jointed dog again rolled the skin back from its teeth, but a kick from Mrs. Denton got Lucy to the car safely.

In Longborough, she made the copies and took the originals out to the street where Mrs. Denton waited in her truck. Mrs. Denton looked over the papers, and handed one back through the window. "Write down the name of the English lawyer, too," she instructed Lucy. "On the back."

"Why?"

"Why? Because I'm entitled. And the address."

She looked carefully at the words Lucy had written, and put the documents in the glove compartment.

Lucy waited for her to drive off. Instead, the woman made it clear she wanted to talk, eventually opening the door and climbing out of the truck.

Lucy pointed across the street. "Want that cup of coffee before you go back?"

The woman nodded and they crossed the street. Inside the restaurant, Nora Denton said, "You're some kind of legal aide, aren't you? You know about legal stuff, I mean."

"What did you want to know? I'm not a lawyer."

The woman looked around the room. "You married?" she asked.

The sudden query, unconnected with the previous question, told Lucy what the woman's interest was in her. Lucy was a married woman who knew her rights. She sought for a good response. "Technically, yes. But I'm separated and soon I'll be divorced." She tried to construct a further opening for the woman. "I left my husband. Walked out."

"Did he come after you?"

"In a way. At first."

"Did he beat up on you much?"

"Oh, no. He never touched me."

The woman was silent, puzzled, and Lucy wondered if she should have lied to encourage her.

"Why did you leave him, then? Was he screwing around?"

"No. I don't think so. I was just unhappy."

"Is it better now?"

"Yes." Now Lucy was silent, rendered sensitive by the woman's questions.

Finally Mrs. Denton asked, "Did you have somewhere to go?"

"I went to a hotel."

The woman drew back. It was the wrong reply. "Okay for some people. What if you had no money? Hotels cost money. What are you supposed to do if you don't have money?"

Lucy felt wary now. Nora Denton's questions had added up to a clear cry for help, but working against the sympathy she felt for the idea of Nora Denton as victim was her disgust at the squalor of the house and especially the kitchen. Now Lucy tried to push aside her own upbringing, telling herself that the fact that Nora Denton was a slattern was irrelevant to the question of whether she was being brutally treated. The one glimpse of the Dentons' life had shaken Lucy. There were various kinds of abuse, she realized. Could she compare her own unhappiness, married to a psychological bully and tyrant, with being married to someone who might at any time smash his fist into your face, or stomach? Kick you? Twist your breast? They say you can get used to anything, Lucy reflected. But not that.

"There are agencies that can help." She pointed to the library. "Ask them over there. They'll tell you where to find the family agency."

"I know where that is. I went there once, and the next day some woman came out to the house to talk to my husband. After she left he beat me up."

"You have any friends nearby?"

"Not nearby, nor far away."

Lucy was cornered. She wrote two numbers on a sheet in her diary and gave the sheet to the woman.

"Here's my home, and here's the office number. Call me anytime," she said.

Chapter 21

"That seems pretty final," Jack Brighton said, scanning the copies Lucy had made. "I'll send them off. Got your expenses?"

"Just the hours. Three would be fair, I think. I don't have any other expenses. I had to be in Longborough, anyway."

Brighton put a sheet of notepaper in front of him and picked up a pen. "How long does it take to drive to Longborough?"

"About an hour and a half."

"So. We're not charging them for a hotel. We'll make it six hours of your time, plus twenty dollars for lunch and thirty for gas. They're still getting us cheap. I'll pay you when they pay me, okay? Now, how's the rest of it going?"

Lucy told him about her project to write a memoir of her cousin. "I want to talk to the bookmaker he bets with. If I'm going to write about him, I have to talk to as many people who knew him as I can find."

"It could be someone not very nice. You know?"

"I just want to ask him a question."

"I know some people. I'll ask around. What happened with that surveillance case of yours?"

Lucy told him how she had spent Thursday evening.

"He want you to carry on?"

"Yes. He says she's agreed to go out every Thursday."

Brighton straightened out a paper clip. "Where do you pick her up?"

"At the Pleasant Boulevard parking lot."

"It still sounds a little phony to me."

"Why?"

"I think you're being set up."

The idea was fatuous. "How?" Lucy asked. "What for?"

"I don't know. He may just be using you as a fishing float. You know, you follow her, he watches you, so the fish can't see him, but he can see you. Like putting a bug on a car. You're the bug."

"But why?"

"Christ knows. Anyway, I'll see if I can find you the bookie."

Before Brighton called back, as Lucy was coming back to her office with some coffee, a client appeared, a small, fat, middle-aged man in a dark suit, a dark tie, and a white

158

shirt. His scalp gleamed through his thin gray hair.

"Mrs. Brenner?"

She nodded, unlocked the door, and he followed her in.

"I'm sorry about Dave," he said when they were both sitting down. "I liked Dave very, very much. I didn't know him too well, though."

"Nobody knew him well, apparently, but everybody liked him."

"That's the kind of guy he was. Warm, but private. My name's Fruitman." He smiled at her suddenly. "How's it going?"

This was such a specious attempt to be agreeable that Lucy felt safe in ignoring it. "Can I help you, Mr. Fruitman?"

He shrugged, spread his hands, lowered them, smiled again, became serious, then leaned forward. "I'm a little worried, Mrs. Brenner. I don't want any problems. Did Dave leave behind some kind of records?"

"Yes, he did. I haven't decided what to do about them yet."

"Burn them, lady. Burn them. They'll only get you into trouble."

"Do you think you are in them?"

"Me? Why would I be in them? Who's interested in Elmer Fruitman? You seen my name anywhere?"

"I haven't read them all yet. Might I find it?"

"Why would you find my name?"

Lucy thought of something. "As a matter of fact, I think I have. Hang on." She turned to the computer and called up the ledger. Fruitman waited restlessly.

"There," Lucy said. "Five hundred, Blue Jays, Fruitman."

"It's a very, very common name, Mrs. Brenner. Very, very common."

"Did the Blue Jays win?"

"What?" Fruitman looked at her as if she was not making sense.

"Did they win? Did you win? Did you pay up?"

"What are you talking about? They lost. Sure I paid up. Doesn't that fucking thing say so?"

"Don't talk like that." Lucy checked the rest of the entries in the ledger. "Not a thing. Forget about it."

"It isn't the money, lady. Not that bet. I know you can't stick me with that. It's a very common name. I made a bet. I lost. I paid. Okay." All pretense was gone now. "It's those fucking records. Excuse me. Look, I'm an undertaker. Business is good. I can handle five hundred, no problem." He reached into his hip pocket and pulled out a wad of hundred-dollar bills and started counting.

"Stop it, Mr. Fruitman. I believe you. You don't have to pay me anything. I'm not going to send a collector round to kneecap you. David's gone. This betting business is all finished."

"Kneecap me?" Fruitman's voice went shrill. "What are you talking about, kneecap me? Jesus, lady, I'm not worried about stuff like that. What kind of business you think Trimble was in? He was a respectable drop. He worked for a bookie with a respectable clientele, like me. Kneecap me. Jesus. You're in the wrong end of town. You're in the wrong *town*. You know what would really happen if I don't pay up?"

"What?"

"Nothing."

"Surely the bookmaker doesn't just forget it?"

"I'm not saying that some bookies don't send round a collector. Not the bookie, the shark, the guy the bookie sells the bet to. It could happen. But not David, not Cowan."

"But if you don't pay . . ."

"All he'd do is cut me off. No pay, no play."

"And that's all?"

"You don't understand. That's the big threat. Then I've got to find another bookie,

161

and he'd be a little rougher. Cowan's a gentleman."

"Another bookie might kneecap you?"

"Will you stop talking about kneecapping? What the next guy would do is threaten me."

"With what?"

"With telling my wife. Then I'm finished."

"Why don't you tell her yourself?"

Fruitman looked round the room, finding himself suddenly locked in with a madwoman. "I swore to her the last time I'd never touch it again. And my son. He's a lawyer, God help me. He could have opened his own funeral home — this business is depression-proof — but he's a lawyer. The last time I was short a few thousand — I'd been betting the Leafs to win — my son, the lawyer, called a family conference. No more betting, they said, or my son would go to the cops."

"He would bring charges against you? Your son?"

"No, lady, he would go to the gambling squad and he would complain, see. They'd listen to him and my wife, too. Then you know what would happen? They'd close me down, tight."

"The police? They would order you not to bet?"

"You don't know anything, do you?

162

"No pay, no play, eh?"

"That's the idea."

"Then it must have been another bookie."

"What bets particularly concern you?"

"Well, none, particularly, as long as he paid up."

Cowan said, "You are a very silly woman. If I was another kind of bookie you might be in serious trouble. I don't know what you are up to but I think you are bluffing. I don't think there's any ledger. I think that you think that you've stumbled onto something."

"Blue Jays five hundred Fruitman on the sixth. Fruitman was in my office. He wants to be sure that David paid you. He's afraid that you'll send someone round to kneecap him."

"Fruitman said that?" Cowan's amusement and disbelief seemed genuine. "Elmer Fruitman said that? I'll pull his leg about that." Then he took out his little book and flipped the pages. "All right. The Jays lost, and David paid. Look." He showed her a small notation in his book: T\Jays 500+2. "That means I gave him two but the Jays lost by five, and that little tick means he paid. See?"

"And if he hadn't?"

Now Cowan looked angry. "I don't want to be bothered with this kind of rubbish,

Where can I start?" Fruitman reamed out his ear with a finger. "See, betting, gambling, is illegal. But it happens. The squad know all the bookmakers, and now and then they drop on them. But the bookies build the fine into their odds, so who's getting hurt? Gambling's legal at the track, but off the track there's nowhere to bet. So take me. I can't go to the track. Someone sees me, tells my wife, and I'm finished. She figures I'm taking bread out of her mouth. Me. I've got a house worth a million and a half, a good business, and if I lost all that I'd still be okay with some other property she doesn't know about. I can afford to bet. She's also afraid I'll be arrested and get in the papers and it'll hurt the business. Hardly likely, is it? She doesn't like the business, anyway. She says it restricts our social life. She won't go to any more undertakers conventions, she says."

"Can you afford to bet five hundred dollars in one go?"

"Sure. I don't waste my money on golf. But she doesn't see it that way. So, I can't bet legally, I bet illegally. You follow? In England I could bet, legally, on who wrote the best fucking novel last year, but here . . ." He raised his hands in disgust. "So what the cops do, they close me down. They put the word out to the bookies. See, the cops don't like my son — he's a lawyer — implying the cops are on the take. So now I can't get a bet on anywhere. Nowhere."

"Apparently all you have to do now, though, is find another bookmaker. Not even that. You paid your bill with David, so your credit's good with Mr. Cowan. Isn't that right?"

"Maybe you don't believe I paid. Maybe David didn't pay Cowan? Okay, I'll pay you again." Fruitman reached for his money.

"Mr. Fruitman, why are you trying to bribe me?"

"Just pay my bet. Here."

"But what for?"

"Take my name out of that fucking machine. That way I know. It's easy. You just type in, 'Delete Fruitman, wherever,' and the machine wipes me out."

"All right."

"You will?"

"Certainly. I don't want you to think the agency is unethical."

"The agency?"

"I'm going to carry on the detective agency."

Fruitman giggled. "That's just a front. Trimble was no bloodhound."

"He worked at it occasionally. Anyway,

I'll make sure no one sees your name."

"Leave me right out of those records?"

Lucy considered telling Fruitman about the impossibility of ever constructing a coherent narrative out of the few scraps she had found so far in the computer. "I promise you that nothing the public is allowed to see will contain a recognizable reference to you. I'll call you 'X' if necessary. How's that?"

Fruitman grinned. "That's great. Then I could read about myself. 'X.' Great. Or call me Fleishman. You sure you believe I paid the bet?"

"Who's Fleishman?"

"He's a prick. Always trying to find out what I'm betting on. Now, that bet . . ."

"Will you stop trying to give me money?"

Fruitman looked unsatisfied again. "Can I do anything else for you?"

Lucy saw that he did not believe they had a deal unless he gave something in exchange. "Perhaps something. First, give me your word that you paid David."

Fruitman looked at her for several seconds. "That's it? My word?" He paused again. "Then you have it, lady. My word."

"How?"

"How?"

"How did you pay him. Like that?" she pointed to his pocket.

Fruitman looked where she was pointing. "Right. Yeah. Five bills."

"Where? Where did you pay him?"

"Right here. Over the desk."

"What did he do with them?"

Fruitman thought about this. "He put them in his pocket."

"When was this?"

"The next day. In my lunch break. Then I went down to the Y for a little workout."

"What day was that?"

"The sixth. Yeah, the sixth."

"And he would have paid Cowan the same day."

"Or the next. No longer."

"What would have happened if David hadn't paid Cowan?"

"Here we go again. Mrs. Brenner, your cousin has been Cowan's drop for a long time. They have a very solid relationship. He would have paid."

"Thank you, Mr. Fruitman. Now, where can I find Mr. Cowan?"

Fruitman gathered his jacket round him and leaned back in his chair. "Why?"

"I want to talk to him."

"I don't know."

"Yes you do. Why won't you tell me? Are you afraid of him?"

"Here we go again. No, I'm not afraid of

him. I just don't want anything to do with him. I dealt with your cousin. That's good enough for me. I don't want to know who he dealt with."

"But you know it's Mr. Cowan."

"That's what your cousin said. But I don't know where he operates from, or anything like that."

"All right. I'll have to try somebody else."

Fruitman didn't move. "We've got a deal, though, eh? You've given me your word. I've done the same. Right?"

"You've got my word. And good luck."

Gradually the tension left him. He stood up, disjointedly. "I don't need luck. I have your word, right? Your word? Thanks, though. If I hear of anyone needing a bloodhound, I'll refer them. Thanks."

Lucy called Jack Brighton. She had a perfect excuse for her first look at the bookie. "I've got David's bookie's name. It's Cowan. Can you find out where his office is?"

Brighton laughed. "I'll see if anyone knows his place of business and call you back."

He called within an hour. "Go to the Ulysses Diner and ask for Ivor Cowan."

"Where is it?"

"On Queen, on the south side, east of Spadina."

"Why, I could walk there. What sort of person is he?"

"He's a bookie-type person. I've never met him. They tell me he's there in the afternoons."

Chapter 22

That evening Johnny Comstock took her to
dinner at Le Paradis, to talk about David
Trimble. They talked about her cousin for
as long as it took to eat the pâté, then they
shared some information about each other.
Comstock tried to give her some idea of
what it was like to be addicted to horses —
it was the only thing he had in common with
Trimble — and how lucky he felt in being
able to live as he did. "I was married once,"
he said, "but it broke up for the same reason
that I probably won't get married again. I
move around a lot, mostly between here and
Kentucky, with rest stops in Florida. But
I'm always working. I like traveling, but I
don't do it for fun. My wife objected that
we never went anywhere she wanted to go.
We did, actually, but not *because* she wanted
to go there. Fact is, if you found me looking
thoughtful on a junk on the Yellow River it
would be because I was wondering who won
the Belmont. That's a horse race. It got her
down eventually. We broke up without too
much blood spilled, though."

In turn, Lucy released the information that she was married, but would not be for much longer, that she lived in Longborough, but planned to move to Toronto, and that she intended to make something of Trimble's detective agency.

"You're on a roll, aren't you?" he said, by way of summing up what she had told him. He explained further. "You're going for it," he said.

Lucy still wasn't sure what he was talking about.

"You feel like taking some chances," he said.

"I suppose that's right."

"It suits you. Makes you give off sparks."

Then Lucy knew that the evening was as much about that as about Trimble. More. Until then it was the farthest thing from her thoughts. It was true that she hadn't fled when The Trog landed on her, but that had been a challenge handed to her by fate, and otherwise life had been a matter of surviving Geoffrey, not looking for more problems. She felt the weight of Comstock's admiration pleasurably, and echoed it, so that later, in the entrance to Trimble's apartment block, when he kissed her good night, she had been thinking for so long, the last hour at least, that he might do that, and wondering how she should respond, how she could get exactly the right message across, that when the moment came she panicked and gave him a quick feverish peck and ran away.

The next morning Peter Tse called in to see her. "You want me to come with you to the bookie?"

"Whatever for? At three o'clock in the afternoon? What can happen? If anything does, you know where I am."

"I thought you might not know the best way to get there. You don't know this end of town too well. I didn't plan to be your bodyguard."

The Ulysses Diner was a fairly new restaurant and bar, decorated to look like an eatery of the twenties, with some neon, a lot of chrome, and curves instead of corners. The bar counter was on the left side of the room, and beyond it a row of high-backed booths offered privacy along the wall.

At three o'clock the room was almost empty; only one of the booths was occupied, but when Lucy started to walk toward it the waiter stopped her. "Lots of free tables over here, ma'am," he said.

"I want to speak to Mr. Cowan. Is that him?"

The waiter looked at her and back at the man in the booth, who was taking no notice of them.

"Ask him," Lucy said. "Tell him Trimble sent me."

"Trimble's dead," the waiter pointed out.

"Yes, well, tell Mr. Cowan I'm his cousin."

The waiter looked at her skeptically, wondering how best to serve Cowan. He looked back, and the man in the booth was looking at them now, so the waiter walked back and whispered deferentially to him. The man nodded and the waiter beckoned her forward.

Ivor Cowan was a tiny, elderly man dressed in a black suit, a white shirt, and a pink, almost patternless, tie. He reminded Lucy of a retired chicken farmer she knew in Kingston, scrubbed and dressed for church.

"Sit down, Miss . . . ?"

"Brenner. Mrs. Thank you for letting me talk to you."

"I'm a bit crowded today, Mrs. Brenner. Can you be quick?"

A waiter appeared and showed Cowan a slip of paper.

Cowan nodded, and the waiter returned to a phone, spoke briefly, and hung up.

"Was that a bet?" Lucy asked.

"It was a message from the lady who cleans my apartment. She's sick. Now, how can I help you?"

"My cousin, David Trimble . . ."

"Ah, yes. I knew David. Lovely man. I hear you're taking over his office?"

"That's right."

"And writing a memoir?"

"I'm thinking of it. How did you know?"

"Word gets around. David recorded his own life story, I hear."

"A lot of it."

"All the people he knew, things like that?"

"Yes."

"My name, for instance? Wouldn't be there. No. I hardly knew him." He looked regretful at the likelihood of being left out.

"I don't remember the names. Did he put bets on with you?"

"That in the memoirs? He was a bit fanciful at times, was David."

"He passed on bets, didn't he?"

"I imagine."

"Quite big ones, some of them."

Cowan said nothing. He took a small book from his pocket and flipped the pages. "Not with me."

Lucy took a breath. "I think I should tell you first that I have deposited a copy of

David's records with my solicitor with instructions that if anything happens to me he is to turn them over to the police."

Cowan took a sip of his coffee and looked at her, concerned. "Do you have a weak heart, Mrs. Brenner? Something like that?"

"You know what I'm talking about. Did David always pay up?"

"He was the type of person who always paid up, I would think. A great guy. Now excuse me. If you need any help with the memoir, I'm often here."

"Oh, the memoir is nothing much. Everything's in the ledger."

"The ledger? He kept a ledger? Do you have it with you?"

"He kept it on a computer. I made a copy of that, too."

"What does it say?"

"Everything. All the bets he made. Who with. Everything."

"Names names, does it?"

"I found yours there."

"Did you? And what do you plan to do with this ledger?"

Lucy took a deep breath. "Can I be honest?"

"Of course. Would you like a drink?'

"A spritzer."

Cowan snapped his fingers, a gesture Lucy

could not remember ever having seen before in Canada. "Bring us a spritzer," he said to the waiter.

They waited for the drink to arrive, and Lucy to take a sip. "Nice," she said.

The waiter said, "We only use imported wine."

Cowan looked at the waiter as if he had suddenly taken all his clothes off, and he disappeared.

"I know David worked for your organization."

"I don't have an organization, Mrs. Brenner. There's just me and one or two helpers. And a few people like your cousin."

"I have to take a chance on you. I'll make a deal with you. Before I do anything with this ledger, I'll take out any references to you. But I want some evidence of your good intentions. Who do you use to collect your debts?"

"What are you talking about?"

"I just want to meet everyone David knew."

Now Cowan withdrew slightly, as if he had just realized he had been insulted. "Look, I'm busy, but I'll tell you this. Go to the police and you'll find out that I don't use collectors. If people don't pay, I forget about it."

ma'am. I don't have any goons, and besides, nobody owes me anything. I made a bet, I won. I think you got what you came for."

His manner convinced Lucy that she had been in serious breach of etiquette. "Sorry. If I find any reference to you, I'll leave it out of the ledger and the memoirs, Mr. Cowan. I may not bother with any of it. But do you have any stories, anecdotes, that I could use?"

"If I think of anything, I'll write it down and send it to you."

"I'll show you the memoir before I send it in."

"That would be best." He put out his hand. As Lucy was gathering herself, he added, "What now? Back to . . . ?"

"Longborough. For the moment, I'm keeping David's office open."

"The — er — business?"

"I'm going to carry on."

Cowan was more polite than anyone else so far, but the expression of doubt on his face was clear.

"You don't think I should?"

"No, no. Of course not. I just had the impression that there wasn't all that much business there."

"It's up to me to build it up, then, isn't it?"

"Won't it be a bit different from what you're used to?"

"I've never talked to a bookie before, either."

"No? Right. I'm sure you'll manage. Good luck, Mrs. Brenner. If any questions occur, about the ledger, I mean, you'll find me here most afternoons. You can tell your lawyer you're meeting me."

"There's one last name I want to check on. Nolan. You know him?"

Cowan paused before he replied, deciding what to say. "I know the name, yes. I believe he bets with a man I know. I happened to be talking to him this morning, and he said that Mr. Nolan had not been around for a few days."

So Nolan bet with Cowan, too. "Did your friend happen to tell you if Nolan had made any bets lately?"

"No. And he would have said something, I'm sure. Is that it now, Mrs. Brenner?"

Lucy stood up. "May I call you if I have any more questions?"

"Here? Certainly. If I'm busy, you can leave a message. I'll get back to you." He nodded politely and returned to his notebook, dismissing her.

There was a message from Johnny Comstock at her office. Would she call him? While she was preparing to, he called again. Would she go with him to Le Select for dinner? It was not far from her office.

"But we just had dinner last night!" It had to be said, this ancient instinct to create a decorous gap between dates in the early stages, not to "rush it," though she was overcome with relief at the news that she hadn't screwed up by running away.

Comstock said, "So we did. But I've just found out I'm going to die."

"When?"

"When did I find out, or when is it going to be?"

"Both. And stop it."

"I found out sometime in the last ten years; it's been coming on slowly. As to the other 'when,' that should happen any time in the next thirty years, sooner if I'm not careful."

"Then what are you talking about?"

"I'm talking about the fact that we are not teenagers, or even young adults — is that the phrase? In other words, we are in the second half, not much time left. So when I find a good thing I don't want to postpone enjoying it on the grounds that we have plenty of time. So can I see you tonight?"

Afterward he drove her back to Trimble's apartment. As they came along Bloor Street Lucy had no idea of what to say when they arrived, or what he would expect. The only experience she had had of dates was twenty-five years old, and Kingston experience at that, and no one in Kingston or Longborough had informed her of the new decorum, whatever it was. She had no doubt where she wanted to be at the end of the evening, or the next one, perhaps, but she hadn't the faintest idea of the conventional way to get there. Even the terms she was rehearsing were probably ridiculous for a woman of her age, at this end of the century, but she had no other vocabulary. Would he "proposition" her? Would she seem cheap if she said yes? Would they spend the whole night together?

He stopped the car outside the block and she waited, but he was no help at all, simply sitting there waiting himself until she knew it was all up to her, and she opened the car door, turned, and said, "Do you want to come in?" And then the old familiar phrase, "It's not very tidy." And then, the truth, "It's kind of crummy, actually."

"Then let's go back to my place."

"I meant, for a cup of coffee."

"There you go again. I didn't."

With The Trog it had been so simple to say yes because he took her by surprise, and anyway she had no investment in the result. This was different. Johnny was no trog; he was someone she couldn't stop thinking about. If she said yes and it turned out badly, she would be shattered. But just this much hesitation was already too much. "All right."

And, of course, there was no question of it turning out badly, certainly not for her, and when he called her the next day to tell her where they were eating that night, she knew that for the moment this was going to be her life.

Chapter 23

It was Thursday and time to get ready to shadow Mrs. Lindberg. She looked at herself, or rather at her new tobacco-colored leather suit in the mirror, and admired what she saw.

Tse put his head round the door and stopped in amazement. "My God, Lucy, you look like a lawyer or something."

Satisfied, Lucy looked down at herself. "You like it?"

"Makes a difference."

"Good."

The telephone rang. "You look terrific," a woman's voice said. Startled, Lucy looked up at the mirror and saw Nina, the travel agent, waving at her from her window across the street. "Now you'll spend as much time in front of that mirror as your cousin used to."

"Probably. Anyway, thanks." That was nice. The only thing that her suit had in common with Nina's red one was that both were made of leather, but Nina might have been miffed. Lucy waved her thanks and got a response from Nina, who raised a fist in appreciation. "You'll have to fight them off," Nina said, and hung up.

Now Lucy wondered if she was properly dressed for work. What she had on was her meet-the-client costume, but she remembered what Lindberg had said when she took the assignment: "You'll do fine." He meant her old image. She needed a disguise. Fortunately she had not yet taken home her original clothes, and she still had a flowered skirt and a cleanish blouse in Trimble's tiny closet. Reluctantly she changed back into the kind of clothes she saw now were likely to be ideal for the job.

Once more, she was ready as the woman pulled out of the lot. She was still nervous, but now only like an actor waiting for his cue. This time they turned north on Yonge Street. Lucy felt herself lucky that the woman was such a deliberate driver — every turn was properly signaled, and she always moved very carefully into the stream of traffic. It makes for excellent practice, thought Lucy, still grim about Toronto driving.

They drove up across Eglinton, where the woman slowed down, obviously looking for a parking spot, finding one opposite the police station. Now Lucy worried that the

183

woman would have disappeared before she found a spot herself — in movies, she reflected, there was always a spot outside Buckingham Palace when the private eye needed it, but the real Yonge and Eglinton was very crowded. Lucy turned at the next side street and scrambled into a spot outside a store that was covered in warnings about what would happen to anyone who tried to park there, got out quickly, and scurried up to Yonge Street before anyone could shout her back. Half a block away, the woman was still locking her car.

There are plenty of pedestrians on that strip on a summer night, and Lucy had no difficulty concealing herself as she followed her quarry half a block south. The woman paused outside a pub, surveyed the street, then walked down into the pub's basement. Lucy gave her two minutes and tried to follow her. She was stopped by a ticket seller in a glass booth. "Three dollars, ma'am."

Lucy had no idea what the charge covered. She was not sure if Toronto had legalized live sex shows, but surely they would cost more than three dollars, so it had to be some kind of bar with a modest entertainment. She paid her three dollars and walked along a passage to a pair of swing doors. Inside was a large room with a rudimentary stage

184

at one end, backed by a fake brick wall. The room itself was in darkness, and Lucy had the time to pick out Mrs. Lindberg, who was seated at a table to the right of the stage, talking to a waiter. Lucy found a quiet spot near the door and ordered a beer, which was what everyone else in the room seemed to be drinking. For a moment she wished she had worn her new suit, for the crowd was casually dressed, convivial, and, on average, about thirty years younger than she.

Quite suddenly, someone at the end of the room began to make an announcement through a microphone, more lights were switched on, and a young man took hold of the microphone and proceeded to tell a string of jokes about the emergency waiting rooms of various hospitals he had visited in his time. Toronto General seemed to be the richest in the kind of scene he made comedy out of, followed by Western. His worst experience had been in England, where the patients sat on a long bench inching eastward until, just before they fell off the end, the doctor saw them. In Paris, he said, they start with a rectal thermometer, then ask you what's wrong. In New York they perform surgery on your wallet (there were boos at the hoariness of this one), but in Naples you get brandy, and maybe an Italian family will

185

take you home for the evening.

All this was delivered feverishly, for laughs, and Lucy rather wished he would slow down because what he was saying, while it wasn't very funny, she found interesting.

When the young man stepped down to not much applause, a young woman took over and the crowd clapped noisily. She explained that she was married to an Albanian and recounted in racist detail how he liked to make love. The crowd applauded every position. Then she explained that she used to be married to a Norwegian, and how he liked to make love. When the girl began to describe the antics, or rather non-antics, of her first husband, an Englishman, Lucy tuned her out. The crowd was grinning at the comedienne, not because she was funny, but because of the atmosphere of the room. As far as Lucy could tell, it was simply a lot of students listening to some of their contemporaries retell anecdotes about things that had happened to them, retelling them in locker-room language, talking dirty as a substitute for wit. Lucy felt like an intruder at a fraternity party.

Another girl took the mike and was genuinely funny about her dog, though not to the woman Lucy was watching, who simply looked slightly to the left and right, apparently not listening.

A voice in Lucy's ear said, "Is that her over there?"

Lucy's arm banged against her beer glass as she jumped away. A hand reached over and pulled the glass back. A man sat down beside her. It was Jack Brighton, the private investigator.

"What are you doing here?"

Brighton grinned, pleased with himself. "Watching the show."

Lucy turned sharply toward the stage.

"Not that one."

It took a moment, then Lucy said, "You mean me and her? You're spying on me?"

"Watch your language, lady. You're in this business, too. Yeah. I've been worried about you."

"For pity's sake. You've been following us?"

"It wasn't hard. You're practically falling over each other. I told you, I've been worried about you. There's something screwy going on. That woman doesn't care who sees her."

"Why should she? Her husband knows she's out. Now go away.

Brighton ignored this. "Same pattern as last time?"

"Will you please go away? Did you follow me from the office?"

"Just from the garage. You told me where to start. I waited in the Becker's lot. Is she on to you, maybe?"

"I hope not. The idea is for her to cope by herself."

"You still believe this agoraphobic stuff? You think an agoraphobic would come here?"

Lucy looked around at the packed, noisy room. "Sure. But what do I know? If not, then what *is* going on?"

"I've been trying to figure it out. You've been staying real close, and if she's spotted you she could act innocent for two or three weeks until her old man runs out of money. Then she could go tap dancing when you're not around."

"Go what?"

"She could do whatever she does when her old man's not around. What he thinks she's doing."

"What are you talking about?"

"I've been reading up about agoraphobia. No way an agoraphobic would come to a place like this. It's the last place."

"Where is it? I mean, what is it? This place?"

"This is amateur night at Yuk-Yuk's.

You've never heard of it?"

"Of course. I should have realized. Then, what's going on?"

"He's having her watched. They may have one of these agreements that let her out on her own one night a week, but he doesn't trust her."

Lucy thought back over last Thursday evening.

"If she knew I was following her, wouldn't she try to . . . shake me?"

"Not if she's smart. It might be me, next time, and she wouldn't spot me. You haven't seen any signs of her shaking you, have you?"

"No, not at all." Then, to prove her point, "Tonight, for instance, after she parked, I couldn't find a space and I had to run into a side street. She had lots of time to disappear. She could just have driven off. But when I came back to Yonge Street she was only just getting out of her car, she didn't look round or anything."

Brighton snickered. "I saw that. I wondered how you would handle it. You know what you should have done? Dumped the car, charged the fine to the client. Or double-parked and stayed in the car until you saw where she went, like I did. I just sat there until I saw you both come in here, then took my time parking."

"But if you hold up traffic out there, everyone starts honking at you. She might have noticed."

"On Yonge Street? She wouldn't have even looked round. Put your emergency flasher on if they honk too much. If you have to, put your hood up."

"I'll remember that. In the meantime, leave me alone."

"Relax. Two of us is less conspicuous. That's her, then, eh?"

"Yes."

"What's she doing?"

Lucy gave in. "I don't know. She doesn't seem to be watching the show. And she's not expecting anyone."

"How do you know?"

"She hasn't looked at her watch. She doesn't look round properly. See, now she's ordering another drink, so she isn't making one last a long time."

"Very *good*. Is she hoping to be picked up?"

"Not among this group, surely."

"Let me find out." Before she could protest, Brighton had moved across the room and was sitting at the woman's table. Lucy saw him say something across the empty seats; the woman turned away from him.

Brighton leaned forward to speak again and the woman picked up her drink and moved to another table. Brighton shrugged and made his way back to Lucy.

"She isn't about to be picked up," he reported.

"Not by you, anyway."

"Not by anybody. She's doing a Garbo. Now she's leaving."

Then Lucy realized that Brighton was half-right, but only half. Suddenly she thought she knew what was going on. She stood up quickly. "You stay where you are," she said. "Call me tomorrow and I'll tell you what she's up to."

On her way out she spoke to the doorman. "That man over there has been bothering me," she said. "Could you stop him from following me out."

The waiter looked at the two quarters she had slipped into his hand. "Give me another dime and I'll have him killed. What d'ya come in here for, anyway?"

Chapter 24

James Lindberg appeared the next morning. Lucy gave him an account of the evening she had spent following his wife's innocent progress, and he put three fifty-dollar bills on the desk. "Plus ten for drinks?" He added two fives.

Lucy swept the money up like a croupier. "Next week?"

He nodded and started to rise.

Lucy squared herself to the desk. She had been thinking about her client for most of the morning and she knew she was right. This wasn't agoraphobia. She had been kicking herself ever since she had realized in Yuk-Yuk's the night before what was going on, kicking herself for not having realized how widespread the problem was. Having lived for most of her life with a man who barred every exit should have made her an expert, and this man was worse than Geoffrey. The woman had obviously fought to get an hour or two of freedom once a week, and Lucy had been hired to make sure she did nothing with it. She said, "You know,

Mr. Lindberg, sometimes she seems to know I'm following her."

"How's that?"

"She does everything so deliberately, as if she's afraid that *she'll* lose *me*." Your wife is not stupid, she wanted to say. This isn't going to work.

Lindberg rejected the message. "Be careful. If she catches on that you're on her tail, she'll panic, and I'll never get her out again. Yuk-Yuk's, eh? That's good, isn't it? I mean, that's a pretty public place. This thing of being deliberate, as you call it. It's natural. It's one step at a time with this kind of thing. She's on the edge of panic the whole time, always wants to run back home."

"Why don't you take her out somewhere nice?"

"I didn't come in here for marriage counseling. I know what I'm doing. Just do it like I say. Keep an eye on her. Okay? It's not dangerous. If you don't want the job I'll get somebody else. But I'm happy with you."

Lucy pretended to give in. "Same time and place?"

"Thursday. Eight o'clock."

She thought about the best way of approaching Mrs. Lindberg. At some point, if the pattern held, the woman would be sitting

193

by herself, in a bar or a restaurant. Lucy would sit nearby, engage her in conversation, being careful not to alarm her, then reveal herself. It was what she said next that was important. Maybe she shouldn't reveal herself, but, if the conversation worked, simply declare herself a fellow victim and hope the woman responded. The important thing was to let her know that comfort, help, was available. And to give her the strength to deal with the creep. If necessary she would offer her the loan of her cousin's apartment for a while.

Unless, of course, the woman liked her situation. There could be some kind of sick symbiosis operating between them, the equivalent of — what was it — S and M? Brighton, she remembered, had been concerned from the beginning, had smelled a rat early. Could it be that it really was some elaborate trap, and she herself the victim? A dozen psychological thrillers ran through her mind. Would she finish up in a dank basement, chained to the wall along with the remains of three other private investigators, her predecessors? Logic, common sense, and courage returned to remind her that it was a long way from Yuk-Yuk's to a dank basement and that she could end her contract the moment her client led her down any dark stairs.

"You'll do fine," the husband had said. Why? Why did she do?

Nevertheless, she decided to find out. By the following Thursday Lucy had made up her mind, keeping her nonsensical fears at bay, and was concentrating on her duty as a woman.

As for her cousin's death, although there was not a shred of evidence that Trimble had been murdered, she had not proved that he had *not* been murdered. A man like Trimble, mixed up with the kind of people he knew, could never, in all Lucy's literary experience, have died accidentally. The fact that she had not found any particular reason why he might have been killed, could (and should) be turned on its head. Such reasons simply had not come to light. Thus, while her common sense put up a struggle against her genre-loaded fancy, she could not resist, from feelings of disappointment as much as anything, picking away at the scab over her doubt.

Her next caller appeared as if to confirm her resolution to help Lindberg's wife.

She had created a file on the Lindberg case, and was just calling it up on the screen when the knock came. She shouted over her shoulder for the visitor to come in and turned to find Geoffrey, her husband, advancing toward the desk.

Lucy watched him sit down, an instinct telling her to gain an advantage by staying silent. He folded one leg over the other and crossed his arms. He was a large, bony, gray man: an old gray suit, large black battered shoes, a worn-looking and greasy tie, gray and black hair and dark jowls on a sunless skin. He looks like a spider, she thought, a giant spider. How did I ever marry him?

"What do you think you are up to?" he began.

It was the worst possible opening for his cause. Lucy had been afraid of a soft question, a smile, an attempted apology, even — it was conceivable — tears. She had felt such a change in herself, slowly over a year, then much more rapidly, that she was very aware of how far she had come from the person he had known, and she had wondered if he, too, might have altered in some way. But his opening question showed that nothing had changed.

Lucy remained silent.

After a very long pause, perhaps a minute, he said, as she guessed he would, "I asked you a question."

"I heard you. I told you the answer yesterday. Now please go away." She bit back the politeness of his name.

"Don't you talk to me like that." His voice rose with him. "I'm entitled to know what you're doing — and who with."

The door opened. "Everything all right, Lucy?" It was Peter Tse.

"Who the hell is *this?*" Geoffrey shouted.

Tse ignored him, continuing to look at Lucy.

"This is my landlord. Mr. Tse. This is my former husband."

Neither man moved.

"And now I'd like you to leave," she added.

Tse came into the room and held the door open.

Geoffrey jumped out of his chair and picked it up, holding it above his head. Lucy backed up into the computer, and Tse took three quick steps round the desk to put himself in front of her. Geoffrey half turned, looked around the room, and threw the chair at the mirror, where it banged against the frame without breaking the glass, then he made as if to tip the desk over onto Lucy and Tse, but succeeded only in scrabbling with his fingertips under the very tiny lip that the desk offered. Finally, he gave a giant kick at the wastebasket, and left.

Tse picked up the chair and set it on its legs and tidied up the paper that had spilled out of the basket. "You all right?" he asked.

Lucy, huddled in her chair, gave a tiny nod.

"A cup of coffee?"

She nodded.

By the time he returned she was more or less together. Tse put the coffee on the desk and turned to the door. "I'll be across the hall if he comes back."

"Do you think he will?"

Tse shook his head. "He's not a fighting man. Did he ever hit you?"

"No, never. I've never seen him like that."

"He was acting. Not dangerous."

She saw immediately that Tse was right. Geoffrey had put on a performance of an enraged, dangerous husband, but it wasn't in him to actually lose control. In the catalog of his faults, that one was missing.

"Yes," she said. "He would never throw the chair at me. But how would you know that?" She shook herself. "That's the last of him, I think. Perhaps it needed that."

"When did you leave him, Lucy?"

"Two years ago."

"After a fight?"

"No. I was gardening at the time."

Tse looked politely incredulous, waiting for more.

It was true that the moment had finally come in the garden. She had read somewhere that Diaghilev's wife used to garden naked when she was well into her eighties, and she was fantasizing imitating her example, just for the pleasure of wondering how Geoffrey would cope with the sight. Lately, it had seemed to her, the smallest attempt at self-discovery on her part brought an instant objection from him. "What do you want to join a choir for?" he had asked. "You can't really sing. I've never heard you mention choir-singing. When does this choir practice? Where? How much time will it take?" On and on and on. It was the same with every single attempt to change their world, from taking off the front porch to serving olives instead of peanuts while they were waiting for dinner. The slightest flutter of her wings brought out his clippers.

Now she leaned over to pick off the head of a peony, still fantasizing playing Mrs. Diaghilev (kneepads, gloves, and a hat — nothing else, she thought: It would probably be like vacuuming in the nude), when Geoffrey spoke from the back door. "I think all this gardening is a waste of time," he had begun. "You can buy them for almost nothing at this time of year."

Deep in her reverie, she jumped sharply at being caught naked, then woke up and became furious.

"Lucy," he called sharply.

"I heard you," she said to the peony, refusing to look up.

"That Almond woman phoned."

Betty Almond was a new acquaintance of Lucy's, her friend, not his and hers.

"When?" Lucy asked.

"They only last a few days, anyway. Why bother?"

"When did Betty phone?"

"The Almond woman? Just now. I told her you were busy. Said you'd call back."

"Why didn't you tell me?"

"You don't have to be at everybody's beck and call all the time. She said something about some plant you might want."

"When did you say I would call back?"

"I didn't. I just said you would."

Lucy continued to address the peony. "You mean she phoned, you looked out the window and saw me in the garden, so you said, 'She's busy. She'll call you back'?"

"More or less."

She took off her gloves and went back past him into the house. Half an hour later she had showered, and she had only to wait for him to leave to play golf. When he returned she was gone.

Now she said, "Yes, Peter, gardening. I'll tell you all about it some time."

Chapter 25

"Peter, what time did you come in and find David? Do you remember?"

"For Chrissake, Lucy, leave it alone. You've got a nice little watching case. You're making the rent. Stick to that."

"Yes, but what time was it?"

"I'm not sure."

"But it's *important*. The police said he had been dead for an hour when they examined him at 9:40. So he died between 8:30 and whenever you came in."

"I can't be too precise. Somewhere between 9:22 and 9:23. I can't get any closer than that."

"All right, all right. How do you know?"

"Every day I take my little niece to the day-care center at Ryerson school."

"Why you?"

"Because I offered. So I can have her to myself for half an hour every day. I don't have any kids. I have two brothers but only one of us is married, and he just has this one girl so we have to share her. I get to take her to school. I have a place to park in the school yard and I get there at five to nine. I leave at nine, when I have delivered her, and I walk here. It takes me twenty-two or twenty-three minutes, depending if the light on Queen Street is red or green."

Tse was grinning, but she pressed on.

"Why don't you park here? It's your building."

"You giving me the third degree? You think I killed him?"

"Don't be silly. I'm just trying to get it all clear in my head and make sure I've asked all the questions, that I haven't overlooked anything." And yet, she thought, none of her favorite detectives would have eliminated Tse, even though you were not supposed to make a Chinese man the villain anymore.

"The parking in the school yard is free," Tse said. "I rent the spaces behind this building for fifty a month. You want to rent one?"

"Is that the real reason why you take your niece to school? To get free parking?"

Tse stopped smiling.

"I'm sorry. I'm a bit upset and taking it out on you. Forget I said that, please. So, if anyone came in they would have to have done it between 8:40 and — what? — 9:15? Earlier. Nina said it was about 9 when she saw him. Oh, hell, it doesn't matter what time you came in, does it?"

"Except for my alibi."

"I said I'm sorry. But no one can get in the building without a key, can they?"

"Right. And the other people already here were Mr. Twomey, the acupuncturist, and Jessie Kwon, the audiologist. It must have been one of them."

Lucy didn't respond. Tse had earned the right to tease her a little. The phone rang. It was Nina. "What about having lunch today?"

Lucy looked up and waved through the window. "I'll be there at twelve."

"Look over first in case I've got a customer. If I have, wait there."

Tse had seen himself out, and Lucy looked round the office for something to do. The phone rang again. It was Jack Brighton. Before he could begin, Lucy jumped in. "I hope you aren't thinking of following me again."

"I wouldn't dream of it. You're too smart for me. Listen, I'm calling about the job you did for me in Longborough. They want you to go back and find some documentary evidence that the woman you talked to is Brian Potter's cousin."

"So there *is* a legacy."

"I guess. Anyway, same terms. I can pay you for the last trip. They deposited in my account."

"When?"

"I'd like a report as soon as you can."

"All right. I'll have the answer in a couple of days."

"Attagirl. How's that other thing going? That woman?"

"I'm still being paid. But I'm going to approach her and tell her what's going on."

"And what's that?"

"I'll tell you later."

"There goes the rent. Don't get too close until you're sure. See you."

"Hang on." Lucy had been thinking. "Could you fax those English lawyers not to write to Mrs. Denton directly, but to use you as a mailing address?"

"I could ask them, but they'd want to know why. Why?"

"I think it would be nice if she got her mail privately. If her husband didn't see it."

"Why?"

"You said there may be money involved."

"What's the name of the game, Lucy?"

"She's the nearest relative, not her husband. If she gets any money she may want to spend it before he finds out. If you'd seen him you'd know what I mean."

"You interfering?"

"I seem to be. Everywhere."

"Okay. I don't see why not. I'll tell them I'll acknowledge receipt of any mail I get from them to be passed on to her. I'll tell them that in our opinion if he sees the money first, then the intentions of the will could be frustrated. How's that? But be careful. We're not social workers, you know. We act on instructions."

"I feel sorry for her."

"I know. That's what I'm saying."

Lucy spent the rest of the morning at the hairdresser in a general effort to look like a successful professional person.

When she came back to her office, Nina was standing in the window, waiting to get together with her.

Chapter 26

Lunch was a Greek salad and a bottle of Perrier. "What I really want," Nina said, "is spaghetti with clam sauce, and bread and ice cream and a big glass of red wine." She patted her tight haunch, sighing. "And a holiday. I've had one day off in the middle of May. That's it for the whole summer. How are you getting on with the sleuthing?"

Lucy told her about the missing boy in Longborough; then, in a rush, she told her the story, now beginning to sound ridiculous, of her suspicions about Trimble's death.

"There wasn't anyone in his office," Nina said immediately. "I think he must have collapsed just before I saw him on the floor. Maybe fifteen minutes."

"How do you know?"

"It's the kind of thing you notice, especially with that big mirror to reflect everything. I came in about a quarter to nine. When I switched on my light he went over and looked at himself in the mirror. I had someone on the phone then for about ten minutes, and when they had gone I got up on the desk *because* I didn't see him around. Then I saw him."

"You climbed up to fix the blind *because* you couldn't see him?"

"I thought he had gone out."

Lucy waited for more. Nina blushed slightly. "When you get back, have a good look in the mirror without moving from the desk. Tell me what you see."

"You," Lucy said promptly. "Oh my. He was watching you?"

"I think so. If I got close to the window he would come close to the mirror. I thought for a long time he was just a vain little man — he was that, too — but he was often looking at me in the mirror. I should have shown him a little flesh."

"The Lady of Shalott," Lucy said.

"Who?"

Lucy explained. " 'The mirror crack'd from side to side; "The curse is come upon me," cried, The Lady of Shalott.' I heard about it in that movie with Maggie Smith about the schoolteacher in Edinburgh. It's about a girl who looked at life only as it was reflected in a mirror, and one day she looked directly out the window and the mirror cracked, and she died." She giggled. "That's what happened. He looked at you without using the mirror one day and the sight was too much for him. Okay, let's leave him alone. I'm still not quite satisfied, but I've got another case to worry about." And she told her friend all about Mrs. Lindberg, ending by saying what she planned to do that night.

Nina listened, then said, "You don't know anything about her, do you? There are a lot of kinky people in Toronto. Be careful. Those two sound a little strange."

"Now *you're* doing it. We've got kinky people in Longborough, too. They all come into the library. I can look after myself. I think she's terribly lonely."

"You think."

"I'm sure. I went through a bit of that with my husband."

Nina waited.

"Didn't I tell you about Geoffrey?"

"This the one who covered you with whipped cream? Sorry. I'm joking. But I can feel a big revelation coming on, and you should count ten before you tell me. No, you haven't told me about Geoffrey or about anyone else."

So Lucy told her all about Geoffrey and why she left him, and how she knew all about being a prisoner, and thus how it was that she recognized poor Mrs. Lindberg's condition. "She's managed to get free for a night a week. He was probably afraid to stop her for fear she would leave him. But the poor woman doesn't know what to do with herself, it's obvious. Just being let out for an airing won't be enough for long. And it's the wrong way. If it's what I think it is, she has to leave him. He's a creep."

Nina moved a piece of lettuce round her plate, picking up the dressing. "You don't think he could be telling the truth?"

"No way. He made that up to keep me quiet."

Her friend chewed and sipped for a few moments. Then, "Lucy," she began, "you know how it is with cars. You tell someone you're having some trouble with your car and she knows right away what it is because she had the same trouble last week, so she tells you to get new shock absorbers or something, but the thing is, there's lots of kinds of trouble that sound alike and when you get to the garage you find out that your carburetor is full of ice or something. You know? People who have a disease can detect it everywhere. I don't mean you may not be right, but be careful."

"You think I may be jumping the gun?"

"It's possible. Don't get too close until you're sure." She patted Lucy's hand. "And after Geoffrey? You're unattached now? I'll never get a better chance to slip that in."

"Yes. Sort of. No. I don't know." And she told her about The Trog.

"Wow! Librarian from Longborough in love nest with . . . what is he? What does he do?"

Lucy had seen the question coming, but not quickly enough. Several seconds passed. "I don't know," she feinted. Then saw that this was the best way of dodging. Suddenly, Ben Tranter's lies sounded ridiculous and Lucy did not want to get into it.

"Stop me when I'm being too personal. You don't know? What does he say he does?"

Lucy had had time now, time to construct what seemed like an artful strategy to avoid Nina's questions. "That's the problem. I only know what he says he does, but I'm not sure I believe it."

"You *are* in the right profession, aren't you? What does he say he does?"

"A mining engineer. He comes to Longborough whenever he's finished a mission — an exploration. He goes all over the world, looking for minerals and stuff."

"But you think he may be lying?"

"Some of the stories have been a bit strange. Like when he comes back from northern Quebec in March with a suntan." She was through the rapids now.

"Is he married, do you know?"

"I've never asked. If he is, he's not happily married," Lucy said, sure that this would sidetrack Nina.

Nina laughed. "That's nice. And he's got a nice thing going with you. Bed and breakfast and you, all for thirty-five dollars? Does he get fresh orange juice for that?" Nina was erupting with giggles.

"Plus tax." This was the right tack. A little modest librarianly bragging and Nina would forget to return to Ben's lies.

Nina lectured the air as if she was quoting, "He's good company, a great lay, and he leaves thirty-five dollars under the pillow. What do I care if he parts his hair in the middle?"

"If he what?"

"I'm adapting something an old friend used to say about her local boyfriend when she went teaching in rural Manitoba. In those days a center parting on a man was the sign of a rube."

"Ben's bald."

"That's it!" Nina cried. "Freud could tell you all about the attraction of bald-headed men."

"Oh, stop it. I'm sorry I told you. So I

don't know much about him, but I'm sure he'll tell me if I don't fuss. In the meantime . . ."

"Don't mind me. It's a lovely story and I won't tell a soul. A year, you say? Don't worry about it. That's enough time to know he's not weird in all the wrong ways. Strange, yes, but not weird." Nina suppressed a further fit. "Listen, if I could find someone like that . . ."

"It's not the sex." Lucy lowered her voice. "Not *just* the sex."

"No. I don't want to be unfair to Geoffrey. Ben isn't a better performer, the way they talk about it now. Sometimes he's so tired we hardly bother, or if we do, we might as well not. You know what I mean?"

Nina, quaking, said, "I know *exactly* what you mean. But Geoffrey was never tired? You started this; I have to know."

"No, never. He took much longer, too, and even when he was finished, it stayed up for ages. I asked him once if it had a bone in it, like bears have. Just joking, you know. But he got angry and told me to behave myself. He was very embarrassed. Are many men like that? Afterward?"

Nina said, "Not in my experience. Oh hell, I don't know what to ask next. How will you know he's coming if you're not

213

there? This trog, I mean."

"I go home most nights, and I have an answering machine."

"Charge him forty and buy a fax. When did you see him last?"

"Not since I came to Toronto. But he's often away for months, looking for uranium or something."

"Don't make it too hard to find you. He sounds too good to be true. It would be a pity if he disappeared before you found out who he is. Now, back to work." Nina scrabbled for money to pay her share of the bill.

"The fact is, now we've come this far, I wouldn't mind if he disappeared."

Nina's search for coins stopped. "Not mind?"

Lucy framed a perfectly truthful observation that was also consistent with what she had told Nina. "Oh, I'd mind a bit. But it wasn't him, you see, but the idea of him. And me saying yes. I'm glad I'm not all tangled up with him, because if he goes away it will still have happened, and now I can move on, do you see? In a way, the less I know about him the better, and I don't think I'll mind if he doesn't come back. I said it wasn't the sex; well, it wasn't even him. Anybody would've done, though it would have to have been someone like him. But now that I've had it, I may not need it anymore. And anyway, I've met someone else." And she told Nina about Johnny Comstock.

She had not fully digested the experience herself yet, but she knew that Nina would have to know at some point because Lucy desperately needed a confidante, and now would do as well as any other time. She hoped Johnny might ask her to go with him to Kentucky or Florida and she would need advice, not on what to say (she would go, all right), but on how to carry herself. She had no difficulty with the morality, but the manners might be a problem.

"My God." Nina stopped making preparations to leave. "A few minutes ago I was beginning to feel it was my duty to tell you what was going on. At that point you sounded to me like the most naïve woman of your age I've ever run into, so I was going to tell you, as a woman of the world, that that trog of yours is obviously a Grade-A bullshit artist who is probably bragging to all of his pals what a sweet deal he's got up in Longborough, how his car broke down one night and he got into this bed-and-breakfast run by this lady who looked like she ran the Longborough Women's Auxiliary but after a couple of bottles of wine she turned into . . . that is, when he asked her,

215

it turned out she was Molly Bloom and now he goes back up for bed and breakfast about twice a month, and they always have dinner first. What was he doing, by the way, with two bottles of wine on his way down from Labrador? They have a liquor store up there on the site? Sounds to me like he carries wine with him, so he would always be ready, like kids in high school with the condoms in their wallets. Hold on, Lucy. I *was* going to say all this, but it's obvious to me now, that while it's all true, what he didn't realize is that while *he* was grinning to himself in the bathroom mirror, *you* were doing the same thing in the bedroom. And now he's done his job and we're moving on to who? Johnny Comstock, horse trainer. Tall?"

"Yes."

"Lean?"

"Yes."

"Suntanned?"

"Yes."

"Gay, maybe?"

And now Lucy felt a blush spreading into her hair, because to answer the question she would have to acknowledge the evenings she had spent in his tiny coach-house apartment in the Annex (his main home was a farm near Uxbridge where he kept the horses not in hard training). After their first night in his apartment, there had been no point in her going home anymore, either to Trimble's ugly little pad or to her house in Longborough. Johnny's apartment was no more than a pad, either, if she understood the term rightly, but it was a nice pad. These days he picked her up every evening for dinner, which they ate early, and then went back there. He had to get up at five, so by ten o'clock they had made love, he was asleep, and she was reading behind a screen at the other end of the room. In the morning he was gone before she woke up.

On the third evening she suggested they stop by an all-night supermarket to pick up some groceries, but he said they would just rot, and she realized that she would have to abandon any nesting instinct she might have. Johnny's flat was, for him, a comfortable place to sleep, to read, to make love, and to watch television. In the morning he made himself a cup of tea, and then ate breakfast at the track. For the second time in her life, the first time as an adult, Lucy was in love. "No," she said. "That is . . ."

"Not gay," Nina nodded. "What about The Trog?"

"Ben was important for helping me to shuck off Geoffrey. Could we drop it now?"

"Sure." Nina, startled by the rebuff, but

ever courteous, found her money again. "As far as this woman you're following is concerned, stay out in the open. There are hidden depths in you, my lady, but you still look like an innocent in some lights. Why don't I come with you?" she ended suddenly.

"I don't need a baby-sitter. But I'm not offended. I think I'm right, too."

"It would be fun. Think about it. No one expects to be followed by two people. If I come with you, no one would dream we were detectives. I'll dress up a bit, and you wear that nice new suit and get your hair done and we'll look like two ladies from Detroit, in for a day's shopping."

"I just got my hair done."

"So you did. It's beautiful, too. I was just making a point."

Lucy was not convinced. I'll dye the bloody lot red, she thought. She saw the sense of Nina's suggestion. "All right. I'll pick you up. Where do you live?"

"Oh, no. I'll meet you there. I know that street. It's opposite a little mall. I'll tell you what. Park your car. We'll use mine. I have a white Ford, a Taurus. You said you have a picture of her?"

Lucy dug it out of her purse, and Nina stared at it. Lucy said, "It would help more if it were full-face, and she never wears those clothes so it's not much use. But then, my guess is that she didn't know he was taking it. He must have taken it indoors when she wasn't looking. Probably phobic about cameras, too."

"Could be. Ten to eight, then."

Lucy returned to her office wondering, not for the first time, why Nina didn't want her to know where she lived, or anything else about her private life. How, for example, could she afford a Taurus? And Lucy remembered that the leather suit was "a present." Was she kept? A rich boyfriend? Somebody's mistress? A high-class call girl? At her age, whatever that was? (Forty-ish?) Not that Lucy cared, she told herself. Whoever it was, he wasn't very demanding, apparently, for whenever Lucy needed her, Nina always seemed to be free. She decided that a trog was the most likely answer, a rich Toronto trog.

Lucy told herself she had to get used to the idea that Toronto people, cosmopolitans like Nina, did not always allow you access to their past. In Longborough you knew everything about everybody, except, of course, the domestic secrets, but in Toronto people came to you with a background full

219

of gaps. It was entirely possible that Nina's job in the agency was no more than a cover for some other more lucrative (and dangerous) activity, money laundering, perhaps, whatever that meant. Perhaps she was a bookie's drop, too, but in that case it would have to be a more upmarket drop than her cousin had been. It was also possible, of course, that Nina lived with a hideous bell-ringer . . .

The phone broke into her dream. It was Nina. For once she was too busy to come with Lucy. "But do me a favor, Lucy. Do not approach her until I'm there, okay?"

Lucy agreed, wondering how many more people would try to look after her.

Chapter 27

As they drove slowly west on St. Clair, Lucy guessed that Mrs. Lindberg was heading for the Italian district that she had heard about. That was fine by Lucy, for whatever sidewalk café the woman chose, Lucy would be able to find one nearby. It was a nice night for a cappuccino.

Then the woman turned south on Spadina, crossing Bloor Street, and Lucy feared the worst, that she was a baseball fan. It would be impossible to watch for her among the twenty thousand Blue Jay fans in the Dome. And then the woman headed for the CN Tower and Lucy relaxed. Mixing up her phobias, Lucy had wondered if the woman would attempt such a test for an agoraphobic, climbing the tallest structure in the Commonwealth. To reach the top you had to travel in a glass elevator on the outside of the building. Lucy's own acrophobia was such that she had no intention of following her, but she had already worked out that all she had to do was wait at the bottom of the beanstalk, as it were; there was only one way down. She had even prepared herself for this with an old paperback copy of *A Coffin for Dimitrios* she had found in the fifty-cent bin of a Queen Street bookseller. The fact that she had read it twice already made it easier to keep one eye on the tower.

But within ten pages the woman came down and they were off again, going east along the lakeshore. It was a beautiful evening for driving along the shore of Lake Ontario; Lucy guessed that they would continue until the woman recovered from being exposed to all the space she could see from the top of the tower, but they stopped at the foot of Bay Street, where she bought a ticket for the island ferry. Now Lucy wondered if she was going to have a problem. Cruising on Lake Ontario on a summer night is a pleasant thing to do, too, and sometimes one of the ferries that serve the islands is hired by a group for a party. They chug around the harbor, a band on the top deck and a bar below, lending a touch of magic to the night, for both the passengers and those enjoying the benches along the shore. And on weekends the ferries are packed with families spending the day on Centre Island, one of the most agreeable excursions that Toronto has to offer. But in the evenings the ferries depart empty from the mainland and bring back the people who have taken a day off, and it would be impossible for Lucy to keep out of sight on the way over. On the other hand, the ferry ride was only the equivalent of the elevator to the top of the tower. There was no other way the woman could return.

Lucy bought a cup of coffee and found an empty seat where she could continue reading her Ambler novel. As each ferry returned, she moved into the shadows to watch the passengers come through the gate; an hour later the woman returned, looking about her in anxious fashion, obviously eager to return to the crowded city.

They drove slowly up Yonge Street, through the hectic street scene below Bloor into the placid lower reaches of middle-class Toronto. It was ten-thirty. Another hundred and fifty bucks.

That week the racing moved to Fort Erie, and none of Comstock's horses was entered so he was free. He picked her up on Saturday afternoon and drove them up to his farm at Uxbridge. As they turned off the county road onto his land and followed the gravel strip up to the farmhouse, she noted how the function of the farm had changed. What must have once been fields of crops were now paddocks enclosed in white picket fences that shouted of horses. The horses themselves, four or five that she could see, ran away as they approached and gathered on a small rise at a safe distance to watch the car.

The house was a hundred-year-old brick building of no distinction, but when they drove round to the back she saw that a big room with a picture window had been added, giving a view over the hills and fields to the west. As they stopped, a small, compact-looking man in his late thirties, dressed in blue jeans and ankle boots, but wearing a tie, came out of the side door to greet them.

"This is Lucy Brenner," Johnny said, "and this is Dennis, Dennis Logan. He looks after the place. Here's Mary, Dennis's wife."

Everyone shook hands. Mary said, "I was just after stocking up your fridge. You're right on time. Come, now. I'll show you in, Lucy, while they have their talk. Bring your bag."

Lucy told herself to tread carefully. She had to figure out the Logans' status so as not to offend anyone or behave clumsily. Were they servants? If so, this was a new experience for her. She had never come across any in Kingston or Longborough.

Mary led her upstairs to a bedroom at the

back of the house. "You can unpack in a minute," she said, and Lucy put her bag on the bed. "The bathroom's right over there," Mary continued, nodding toward the hall. "Ours is on the other side of the house. Oh, look, I assumed you were sleeping together. There is another little room if you want it?"

Lucy moved to the window with her back to Mary, blushing as lightly as she could. "No, no. Yes, this is fine." She turned and looked round the room. There was a large double bed, high off the floor, an old but valuable-looking chest of drawers, a chintz-covered armchair, night tables with reading lamps on either side of the bed. The room was so simply furnished that a chamber pot under the bed seemed possible. Lucy moved over to the chest of drawers, then paused, not sure of her rights.

"The top drawer is empty," Mary said. "I'll leave you now. Come down when you're ready."

A woman's voice called to them from downstairs. Mary shouted a hello from the landing and ran down to meet the caller, as Lucy realized her purse was still in the car and began to follow her down. She stopped on the top of the stairs long enough to hear Mary say to the newcomer, "He just arrived. I was just showing his latest their room. Yes, wait and meet her." Lucy continued down, coughing noisily, and Mary introduced her to the neighbor, a Mrs.-Wiggs-of-the-Cabbage-Patch who was apparently delivering the week's eggs.

When Lucy had collected her purse and spent enough time in the bedroom to have done whatever visitors were expected to do — take a nap? take a bath? change her clothes? (but she had traveled in her L.L. Bean look, which seemed right for four o'clock in the country) — she went down to the living room.

"Cuppa?" Mary asked, from the couch.

Lucy nodded, and Mary poured out the tea and held the cup up for her.

Not servants, then. Servants in *Upstairs, Downstairs* didn't serve sitting down.

Lucy sat in one of the chairs and drank her tea and looked out the picture window at rural Ontario. It was a gorgeous scene: The farm was almost entirely given over to meadows, surrounded by the equally green fields of Johnny's neighbors, varied slightly by the occasional field of golden stubble.

"What do they grow?" Lucy asked. She was determined not to make remarks about how pretty it all was at this stage, but to generate a response.

"Mostly their own hay for their children's

226

ponies. These are all hobby farms owned by rich stockbrokers who need a tax loss. Beautiful view, isn't it? Shows you what God could do if he had the money. I read that somewhere." Her tone was easy, rendering the hobby-farmers risible and unthreatening.

"Except for Johnny."

"Except for Johnny, what?"

"You said they were all owned by stockbrokers. Except for Johnny."

"Well, he's not one anymore, but he made his pile on Bay Street, you know, before he took this up. You can't make the kind of living he enjoys, training horses."

Tuck that away, Lucy thought. Don't push it. She nodded. "I like your living room," she said, changing the subject to indicate either her total lack of interest or her full awareness of the secret of Johnny Comstock's fortune.

"This is Johnny's. Didn't he explain? Let me show you round. It'll be easier." She led them through a side door. "See here? This little pantry. This is Johnny's kitchen. He just put it in a couple of years ago, when he started using the place the way he does now. Now across the hall here is *our* living room, mine and Dennis's. Walk down this passage and you come to . . . this." She opened a door onto a kitchen like an advertisement in an English magazine aimed at rich rustics. As well as the quarry-tiled floor, the polished pine tables, the marble kitchen counters, and the rows of herbs on the windowsills, the kitchen was surrounded on three sides by casement windows open now to let in the scent of Comstock's own new-mown hay, and beyond lay a beautifully cobbled yard set with an apple tree on one side and what looked like a Japanese garden on the other.

"I just finished making the garden," Mary said. "Do you think it's all right, here in Canada?"

The emergence of this mild doubt, the appeal to Lucy's taste or superior Canadian-ness, or whatever, eliminated any distance between them. Lucy had long come to terms with the fact that as well as being unable, really, to cook (not counting the steaks and stews that Geoffrey had expected), or knit, or sew, she had no aptitude for interior decoration whatever, although she liked polished floors, firelight, rugs on bare floors, and pictures with people and buildings in them, and she was maturing, she knew, having recently gone off pewter, so she had not looked critically at the scene before her. Now she tried and it still looked as agreeable. "I think it looks marvelous," she said, that and no more because she knew that she could blunder trying to comment on the garden. It looked Japanese, but it could well be the newest outdoor decor from Taiwan, not yet seen in Longborough, but available in a kit from IKEA.

Mary led her round the outside of the house, pointing out the flowers, which were grown for cutting, and the vegetable patch, and they came back to the living room. "So there you are," Mary said. "Like it? Oh, look." She pointed through the window at the car disappearing along the road. "They've gone to see a man about a horse. Let's have a drink. Come back in the kitchen. I've got some tonic cold."

When they were settled on stools with their gin and tonics, Mary said, "First of all, this all belongs to Johnny. My husband works for him, manages the horses and what's left of the farm. We're from Ireland, did you notice?" She laughed. "When Johnny bought this place to keep the horses not in training, he needed someone to run it, and word was passed and Dennis flew over and got the job. It suits him perfectly. I won't tell you his background, but it's what he's trained for. But the money went out of his family and Dennis was about to become a brewery representative, a traveler in light ale, no less."

Mary seemed to have stopped, and Lucy nudged her deliberately in the wrong direction to get some information. "So Johnny and Dennis are partners?"

"No bloody way. Dennis works for Johnny. He's Johnny's employee. And in case you're wondering, I *don't* work here. I teach school in Uxbridge. Today, and on other days like this, I just make myself agreeable."

"To all of Johnny's women?"

"Ah, yes, well, you heard that, did you? Sorry. But some of the people Johnny brings up mistake me for the housekeeper. I'm not. No, no, let me finish. This is Johnny's house, which means he's the proprietor, but it's our house to live in, and this is my kitchen. It goes with Dennis's job. But Johnny likes to come here to spend time, a couple of days, usually, so he built his living room on and fixed up another little kitchen and a second bathroom so he wouldn't be squeezing us when he came. He did most of it himself. We use his sitting room sometimes when he's not here, but we're pretty comfortable without it. I'm nearly finished. We don't share. When they come back from seeing that horse, I expect Johnny will take you into Uxbridge for dinner. There's a little freezer in your kitchen with some frozen dinners in it if you want, and I've put some bread and milk and eggs and bacon in the fridge so you can cook breakfast. If you want to make a salad you can take what you want from the garden out back. There's dressing in the fridge. I think that's everything. Now I have to run. We've got company for dinner."

Lucy sat looking at the manicured land-scape, thinking, Johnny's latest, that's what I am. I ought to be a lot thinner than this, surely. With blond streaks. He probably likes a change, though. That's me. Johnny's latest. Latest what? Girlfriend (the second in three years)? Piece of strudel (the third this month)? Tart, then? No. Somewhere in-between? Probably. Lucy tried out all the variables and came up with one that suited her. I'm Johnny's latest attempt to find the woman he wants to spend the rest of his life with. How about that? And what was he to her? Her latest? It wasn't even gram-matical if he was only the second. But he *was* her latest, latest in the sense of the most recent attempt by her to discover what the world had to offer.

She heard a car door slam, voices, steps, and Johnny padded into the room in his socks. "My boots are dirty," he said. "Pour me a large Scotch with an equal amount of tap water, and I'll put some dry shoes on and take you out to dinner."

After dinner they came home and played Scrabble until she felt the inside of her head tip over, and he laughed at her and sent her up to bed while he finished reading something. She tried to stay awake in case he wanted her at the end of the chapter, but she never heard him come up. The next morning when she opened her eyes he was already awake with his hands behind his head. He kissed her interrogatively and she responded affirmatively.

Afterward, she thought, I can't cook, I'm no house-and-gardens person, I can't play the piano, or sing, and I don't know anything about horses. What does he see in me? She said, "Where do I stand? I need to know."

He didn't pretend to be puzzled, to take time to understand her question. "I brought you up here to ask you the same thing," he said.

But the initiative was hers, and she hung on to it. "I'm your latest," she said. "I know that. Latest what, though?"

"Who said that?"

"Latest *what?*" she repeated, sitting up.

He sat up beside her. "Not the latest. The last, I hope."

"What does that mean? No soft soap, now."

"I'd like to keep you. For good."

"Me move in with you, you mean?"

"That's it."

"Why?" It was nearly a cry.

"Christ. Where shall I start? Okay, I like the feel of you."

"You mean like, just now?"

"That's it. But now, too." He ran his hand across the bottom of her back. "And I like the look of you, too."

"Ah, come on."

He lay down again. "All of you is in your face. Most people walk around with a mask on, but you don't. There's more going on in your face than I've seen on anyone for years. And you make me laugh. So there it is: Seeing you makes me smile, and hearing you makes me laugh. How's that? Will you stay? If so, I'll make some breakfast. Whenever you're ready."

He scrambled some eggs for them both and then told her to amuse herself for an hour while he went for a ride. She went up to the bedroom to watch him through the window as he and Mary cantered around the field behind the house, while Dennis watched and shouted remarks. For lunch he proposed they drive to Stouffville, where he knew of a pub, but she offered to fix them some grilled cheese sandwiches, which he said were his favorites, so that afterward she could ask him to teach her to ride, unless he thought she was too old, or too fat. She did like horses, and wasn't afraid of them.

Johnny said, "Well, that's a start. What size are your feet?" When she told him he disappeared into the back of the house and returned with a pair of ankle boots and a hard hat. "Who owned these? Your last-but-one? Or do you keep a supply, like spare toothbrushes," she still wanted to say, but she kept quiet long enough for him to tell her they belonged to Mary, and they went out to the barn, where Dennis helped him saddle a pair of horses.

She was glad the one intended for her looked old and sleepy, if rather big. Dennis showed her how to mount, and she wobbled forth, knees clenched, the rest of her swaying, trying to find a point of balance. Mary came running from her kitchen and busied herself tightening buckles and adjusting stirrups, and the two riders walked their horses around the field.

He kept them out for an hour, talking at her all the time, and at the end she could make her horse start and stop and trot. When they came in, Dennis showed her how to dismount and caught her when she found her legs were paralyzed. When she was steady, she started to walk to the door and Johnny called out, "Where are you going?"

"Leave her now," Mary called from the door of the barn. "I'll do it."

"She should do it herself," Johnny said.

"I'll do it," Lucy said. "If I can. What is it?"

Then Mary showed her how to unsaddle the horse and remove the bridle, how to brush it down, to clean its feet and put it in the loose box. All of which left Lucy exhausted, aching, stinking of horse, and very pleased with herself. She could do this. The feeling persisted. Even after a shower and a drink, she still could not remember feeling more pleased with herself.

Chapter 28

Tse poked his head round the door. "Busy, Lucy?"

Lucy picked up a sheet of paper, headed CASE #2 — THE LONGBOROUGH MISSING PERSON. "Lots of work," she said. "Some more, anyway." She turned back to her desk. "Thanks, Peter."

Tse took the hint and left. Lucy looked round the room for something to do and decided to have another go at retrieving Trimble's diary.

"I fink he would've written it down, like he would his bank machine number," she remembered Tse saying. Where? When? When he bought the computer, when he would've read the handbook and found out the way to keep a file secret.

She moved awkwardly to the file cabinet, her thighs still aching, drew out Trimble's folder of income tax receipts, and emptied it onto her desk. There it was: the receipt. May tenth. So, on May tenth, eleventh, or twelfth, or somewhere in the next few days, he wrote down the code word. Where? What would he have been looking at when he set it up? The manual. But did he set it up himself?

She walked over to Tse's office and asked the landlord.

He tried to think. "He worked at it all day when it came. Then, wait a minute, he got someone to come in and show him. Why?"

"Just wondered." She returned to her office and now found it almost immediately. A sheet of computer paper, taped to the wall above the machine, on which were the elementary instructions for switching on the software. She had looked at it a dozen times a day without reading beyond the first line, being familiar with the instructions.

"Switch on both," it began.

The screen and drive, Lucy thought.

"Wait for dee-dee-dee-. Type 'cd\wp50' and 'Enter.'

"Now type 'wp,' then 'Enter.'

"Wait for it, then press 'F5' twice. Roll down the light to the file. Press 1.

"Don't forget to save."

Then, in pencil, was written, "For Diary use bank machine access #."

"That's it," Lucy shouted. She pulled open the desk drawer and found the wallet, tore it apart to get the slip of paper in the "secret" compartment. Then she turned to the machine and ran through the ponderous instructions, arriving at the highlighted DIARY, then typed "6205" and "Enter."

The screen sprang to life. "Old smartypants," Lucy said.

"You or Dave?" Tse, who had appeared behind her, said.

"Both."

"What's it say?"

The diary began,

Nina's had her hair dyed. Suits her. I love watching her put on lipstick. I don't think she uses any other makeup. What scent does she use? Is there such a thing as cucumber scent? Cool and green? There should be for her.

There were several pages of this, all about Nina, all of it adoring without being distasteful. It ended,

She's away today. I called her office when she didn't appear. She might be sick.

Then,

She's back. Looks a little tired but still . . .

The text broke off and something else started.

Fearful of how her cousin's fantasies might develop, Lucy switched off the machine.

"What are you doing?" Tse demanded, furious at having his reading interrupted.

"It's a diary. Private."

"But *you're* going to read it!"

"I'm his cousin. In the family. Now leave me alone."

"That's not fair!"

"I know. But that's the way it is. Off you go now."

When Tse had gone, she locked the door and switched the machine back on, finding her way to the diary, and settled down for a good read. But three pages later the story of Nina ended, still adoring but still without raising a blush.

The diary material was followed by a cryptic entry:

June 1: MacGovern said today Sly Peek should be good for the 7th. Nolan says he can get the drugs.

June 2: Comstock says Desk Lamp will run. Find out who's on Sly Peek. Get

239

him to strangle it until Desk Lamp appears. Pay him odds to 500 on Desk Lamp.

June 3: No good. MacGovern worried. Getting Billy Woodhouse up on Sly Peek. Have to use Mac himself. Tell the boys he's betting against himself, on Desk Lamp. When Cowan hears that he won't lay off.

June 4: Comstock says we can't risk bringing Mac in. He talks. Pay him off after.

June 5: Got the drugs. Green for fast, red for slow. Nolan wants to be sure, so he'll do the injections himself. Beautiful. Already switched the labels. Mac worried. Could lose license. But Nolan guarantees drugs undetectable. They're from Hong Kong.

June 7: We're on. 5000 on Sly Peek at track odds. Comstock supplied the money. Cowan took it because there was plenty of time to lay it off. His information was that Mac was betting on Desk Lamp.

(Later, same day) Cowan knows

he's been had, but he'll pay up. He's got his reputation to consider. Bookies shouldn't gamble. Nolan is suspicious, but by the time he figures it out, I'll be gone. Told Mac the whole story and promised him 25 Gs.

June 8: Cowan paid up. He's making enquiries, though. Stewards were unhappy, it says. Comstock says he can handle the enquiry. 500 bills makes a nice little bundle.

Now the entries stopped and a new fantasy about Nina developed.

The significance of what she was reading sank in before she understood the whole story. Once more literature had prepared her to recognize the pattern. All those stories hinging on the discovery of the real man behind the respectable mask, ranging from, at worst, the realization that your dentist is the serial killer much sought after by the police, through incest, to the less horrible but more interesting discovery that you are only one of your husband's wives, raising only some of his children.

This discovery belonged at the more alarming end of the spectrum. At the very least, Johnny was a swindler. Lucy tried to rationalize it away by telling herself that in his world swindling was the norm, but she stuck at the point of all the honest people who had bet on Desk Lamp that day.

Worse, akin to the discovery of the rotting corpse in the basement, was the possibility that he was a thief, involved in robbing her cousin after Trimble had collected from the bookmaker.

She also forced herself to consider that Comstock was an actor in Trimble's death, and decided it made no sense at all. She *knew* there was no violence in Comstock, never mind the rest. If Trimble's death was not natural, it was much more likely that an injured party was involved. There was no reason for Johnny to attack her cousin, and if he was a thief, it was only because Trimble had died.

Swindler and thief were enough, though. Now what? She was in love with a no-good. It was possible that Johnny could "explain," but the presence of all the names — Johnny's, Cowan's, MacGovern's, Nolan's — gave the account a terrifying authenticity. And if he was a swindler and a thief, he was also an accomplished liar. Before she confronted him, if she ever did, she needed to make herself an expert on the case.

The obvious person to consult was Peter

Tse, but some delicate desire to protect her dead cousin's name, at this stage, anyway, made her want to keep the problem to herself, to try and make sense of it on her own.

It was easy enough to make a start. Every item in the entry was dated, leading up to the day that the bet was placed, the day of the race. It took her an hour to drive to Metro library, borrow the *Star* for June 8, photocopy the results of the day's races at Woodbine, and return to her office and lock the door.

Sly Peek had won the third race, at odds of ten to one; Desk Lamp, the favorite, was among the also-rans. There was no other information that she could check against the diary. The jockeys were named — Woodhouse was on Sly Peek — but not the trainers. She ran downstairs to the smoke shop and bought a copy of that day's *Racing Guide* and confirmed that it contained the names of the trainers; she had only to find a copy for the day in question. This, too, was easy — a phone call to the paper's offices, a promise to photocopy what she wanted if she came by the office, and she was driving across the city wondering what she would do with the information if it checked out.

★ ★ ★

The *Racing Guide* listed the trainers: Johnny Comstock had trained the badly beaten favorite, Desk Lamp, and MacGovern was Sly Peek's trainer. There was a small news item about a stewards enquiry that had been held about the running of Desk Lamp, but the stewards had been satisfied with Comstock's explanation.

What about Johnny? Lucy thought. Was he satisfied?

There was still much that she didn't know, but she set herself to decode what she could. Evidently two horses had been drugged, one to run fast and the other to run slow. Sly Peek had run fast and Desk Lamp had run slow, that was clear enough, and evidently Desk Lamp had been the favorite, at two to one. The swindle involved Johnny, the trainer MacGovern, and the man called Nolan, the one who procured the drugs. But if Nolan was suspicious, both before and after the race, and MacGovern was eventually not let into the final steps of the swindle, but was told the story afterward and paid off with twenty-five thousand, then evidently there had been a double-cross involving Trimble and perhaps Comstock. That must be what "switched labels" meant, that Trimble had managed to switch the labels before

244

giving back the drugs to Nolan. Trimble, MacGovern, and Nolan had therefore conspired to make sure Desk Lamp won, but by switching the drugs, her cousin had assured himself that Sly Peek would be the winner. MacGovern and Nolan had backed Desk Lamp, of course, and when the bookmaker heard that the trainer was betting against himself, he decided not to "lay off" (pass on?) Trimble's bet. He would be assuming that Trimble's information was not as good as his own.

The little subplot involving the jockey was unclear, but that could wait until she learned a bit more about horse racing. She thought for a long time about what she had learned, but it only became clearer: In its simplest form, David had won fifty thousand dollars, which was either still in the office or the apartment or had been found by whoever broke into the office, possibly by someone who knew it was there, Cowan, or Nolan, or MacGovern, or Johnny. Nolan, she remembered, hadn't been seen for a few days. Now what?

The telephone rang, but she ignored it, needing time, in case it was Johnny, to decide on a response. It would have been bad enough to discover that Trimble had been involved in a piece of crookedness like this;

to find Johnny involved was to make nonsense of the future she had been constructing, a future in which he was already central. Lucy felt like running back to Longborough and asking for her old job back.

But as she sat there, ignoring the telephone, she knew that she was going to have to tell Johnny what she had learned about him, the reason why she would not be seeing him again. And there was still the possibility that her cousin had been murdered by someone who knew he had fifty thousand dollars. She could not just walk away from it.

Chapter 29

The first thing was to find some flaw in her discovery, something that would bring the world and Johnny Comstock back to normal. There were still things she did not know about horse racing, and while the story on the computer looked pretty definitive, locking up the details was something she could do while she got used to the sickening idea that she would not have Johnny Comstock in her life in future.

The phone continued to ring, six or seven times. Each time she let the answering machine cut in, and each time it was Johnny trying to find her.

The novels that Trimble had accumulated provided a starting point. She picked out a Dick Francis and placed it open in front of her on the desk, putting the *Racing Guide* and the diary printout into a drawer. Then she unlocked the door, left it slightly ajar, and waited.

Peter appeared in half an hour. "Watcha doin', Lucy?"

She held up the novel.

"Doesn't look too good if a customer comes in."

"You're the only one who doesn't knock."

"Don't leave your door open, then. Hungry?"

"I guess so." Then with elaborate casualness, "You read Dick Francis?"

"I haven't got time for novels." The classic answer, irritating usually, but now the one she wanted.

"You should find time, you might learn something. These, for instance. Most of them are about racing, although I sometimes feel I'm missing something because I don't know enough about horses. One I read the other day, for instance, was all about how a race was rigged."

"Which one? Let me see it."

"It's at home. I wouldn't have thought it was possible."

"It happens. How did they do it?"

"They drugged two horses. One to go fast and the other to go slow."

"Complicated."

"But how could they be sure they'd win? There were seven other horses in the race."

"They couldn't be *dead* sure. They'd have to get every trainer in the race to cooperate. You can do that in harness racing, I've heard. If an owner-driver is down on his luck the others let him win a little purse, just to keep him going. See, with harness racing they all go round and round in single file until the last little bit. You can't tell who's trying."

"Does everybody know this?"

"Nobody *knows* it, Lucy. It's what I think when my horse comes second."

"Never mind about harness racing. Let's stick to the other kind. The kind in the novel," she added.

"Thoroughbreds. Why don't you answer your phone?"

"Because there's someone I don't want to talk to. You don't think thoroughbred owners all get together and agree who should win?"

"It's not possible. Not all of them. A couple might. Two or three maybe. But not all of them. More likely someone interferes with the favorite. Some of the horses in each race are just running for exercise. Everybody knows that."

"Do the people who are betting know it?"

"Some of them. Anyway, nothing's certain. If you see a horse win at fifty to one, then the owner and trainer didn't back it. It was just running for exercise, but that day it felt good, literally feeling its oats."

"Or it was drugged."

"If they catch a trainer giving a horse drugs, he loses his license. They test the winner of every race. Look, let's go down and have a coffee, and I'll explain it a bit."

Over coffee in the Portuguese restaurant, Tse tried to lay out the elements of racing. How a trainer can perfectly legitimately, or rather, without much fear of detection, hold up a good horse for several races until the price is right, then let it win at nice odds. How he can switch around the equipment — blinkers, tongue-strap, noseband — to affect the running of a horse; how a jockey can give a horse a poor ride while seeming to do his best; how, in short, a trainer and a cooperating jockey can make a horse win them some money without the whole world knowing what is going to happen first. All this and much more Tse told her.

"And this is all legal?"

"Not *legal*. Every horse is supposed to run his best every day. But it isn't crooked, either."

"But drugs are crooked?"

"Some are, sure. But you have to catch them. Trouble is, the boys with the drugs are one step ahead of the vets. Every time they test for a new drug, the boys are already using something else."

Indeed they are, Lucy thought. "Why do people bet? With all this going on, their horse might not be getting a fair chance."

Tse laughed. "Like the man said about the poker game, 'I know it's crooked but it's the only game in town.' What I'm telling you everybody knows, so you try to figure out what they are doing and bet accordingly. You remember when we were out at the track you told me about that old lady whose horse was running? I looked it up, remember, and although it had been losing, that trainer, Johnny Comstock, had put it up against better horses. I figured he'd decided to win one for the old lady, and he had been getting it ready. I was right."

"But it didn't win. I bet that horse to show because she was such a nice old lady."

"It came second by a neck, but it was *trying*. What more can I ask? I lost my money but so did the trainer and the old lady."

"Another thing," Lucy continued, trying to look like someone who was puzzled by a detail in Chapter Eight, "if a bookie gets a big bet, what does it mean to say he lays it off?"

"What it says. He just turns round and bets with a bigger bookie, to cover himself. That way he'll probably earn a little commission, service the customer, but he won't risk losing a packet."

"But if he's sure the horse will lose, then he might not lay it off?"

"That's called betting, gambling, and bookies don't like to gamble. But he might, if it's absolutely safe."

"If he heard, say, that the trainer was backing someone else's horse?"

"That might do it. Then, depending on the trainer, he'd know that it wasn't trying, that the jockey might hold it up."

Lucy shook her head. "And yet you *still* bet."

Chapter 30

With the help of Tse's instructions, Lucy once more compared the diary with the *Racing Guide*'s version of the result. Once more she felt the necessity to speak her thoughts aloud, but not to Tse. She had caught a flicker of curiosity from him when she had momentarily forgotten that she was supposed to be talking about the plot of a novel: She didn't want to arouse him any further. There was only one person. She picked up the phone and dialed Nina, waving to her through the window as she identified herself. "I need help," she said. "Are you free for dinner? I need you."

"How important is it? I have an appointment."

"Oh, Nina, it's very important. To me."

"Sure. Straight from work? Where are you taking me?"

"That place you showed me the other day. I'll see if I can get a table at the end. This is very private."

"Sounds a lot more interesting than getting my feet done. Pick me up when you're ready."

* * *

Le Select had a table available in the corner of the front room where they would not be overheard. Lucy pulled out the diary and the *Racing Guide*. She had made an extra copy of the diary, snipping off the surrounding text that contained the fantasies about Nina. Step by step she took Nina through it, having to explain every detail because Nina knew nothing about horse racing. By the time the coffee arrived, Nina claimed she understood what Lucy was talking about.

"There's a story there all right," she said. "Your cousin and your lover managed to fix a race and made, my God, fifty thousand dollars."

"And David got killed for it. By Nolan or Cowan, or Johnny."

"Don't go off half-cocked . . ."

"But it's all there!"

"David died of a heart attack, right in the office. I saw him."

"You didn't see who was there earlier before you came in. And he might have had a phone call, saying they were coming for him, or have been looking out the window and saw Cowan's enforcer come into the building. You can't get round this." She slapped the papers on the table. Her voice had risen slightly as the hysteria she was controlling bubbled through.

Nina pressed her hand. "It looks like something bad, all right. But be careful. They sound like a lot of . . ."

"I know. But there's fifty thousand around somewhere. That's what they were looking for when they broke into the office. I knew it."

Nina said, "Can I go over it again to make sure I understand? There's Desk Lamp last . . ."

"At two to one. Someone must have been backing him or he would have been at four or five to one."

"Let me do it, Lucy."

"Sorry." Lucy dabbed the corner of her eye.

"Sly Peek — there's a name that would have appealed to your cousin — won at ten to one, therefore his trainer wasn't backing him. Right?"

"MacGovern."

"And even the stewards thought that Desk Lamp had run badly. What are you going to do?"

"Find that fifty thousand dollars. Someone tried to rob him after he was dead. Cowan paid up, so David got the money. I think it might still be around because they searched everything and if they'd found it, I would have seen where their search ended."

"Clever. If you find it, who does it belong to? You?"

"David got it by cheating, so I can't keep it."

Nina blinked. "You could give it back to that bookmaker. He'll be pleased."

Lucy shook her head. "He thought that the race was rigged for Desk Lamp to win, so he shouldn't benefit. Serves him right for trying to outsmart David."

"The Salvation Army?" Nina looked at the race result again, and pointed to a line. "What does *that* mean?"

"It means the race was worth forty thousand dollars."

"So if Desk Lamp had won, as it should have done, then that owner would have won forty thousand dollars?"

"Say thirty. The next three horses get some."

"What an expert you've become! Him, then, for a start. What about Nolan, and the trainer of Sly Peek? They lost their money."

"Don't make fun. They're all crooks. They deserve what they got."

"Then pay Desk Lamp's owner, and take the rest as your fee."

Lucy considered this. "Actually, that seems fair."

"Don't spend it yet. Find it first."

Lucy remembered an early piece of advice from Jack Brighton. "I ought to go to the police now," she said.

"You're not going to, though, are you?"

"I'm going to have another look for the money first. And I think I'll just go and see that bookmaker again. Make sure he paid up. The diary isn't clear about that."

"Then what are you going to do?"

"What? Oh, I don't know." As the subject finally came up, Lucy's eyes filled with tears. "I can't believe it, Nina. A crook? Johnny? But what else can I think?"

"I wish I'd met him. I would know."

Lucy said suddenly, "I'm not going to accuse him before I'm sure, and even then I'll have to get used to the idea, if you see what I mean. There's no rush. Nobody knows what I've found. I have other work to finish, and then I'll come back to it, when I'm less upset."

"That sounds right."

Chapter 31

She began at the bank. "I want to have a look at five hundred one-hundred-dollar bills," she said to the assistant manager. It was not the kind of thing you could say to a cashier.

"You want to know what five hundred hundred-dollar bills looks like?"

"Yes."

"Apart from the color and the pictures, the same as five hundred one-dollar bills. Of course, the one-dollar bill is phased out now, but five hundred two-dollar bills would look the same, better, closer in color to hundred-dollar bills. Why?"

"I'm researching a television show. We want to show the ransom money."

"Yes?" The assistant manager, a Japanese man of about twenty, looked pleased. He disappeared, reappearing with a woman in her fifties who looked as if she enjoyed having her leg pulled by the Japanese man. "You really want to see five hundred two-dollar bills?" she asked.

"Yes, please. New ones, I think."

258

"For a television show," the man said. "They want to show the ransom money."

"Who's being ransomed?" the manager asked, as pleased now as the man. "You want to bring the cameras in here?" She looked at the man. They both giggled slightly.

"I just want to see how big five hundred bills is."

"About so big." The woman lifted her hand an inch off the counter.

"Bit higher," the man said, raising the woman's hand.

"Now, Jim," the woman said. "Go and see to my customer. Come in," she said to Lucy. "I'll show you."

She stopped Lucy at the door of the vault, disappeared, and returned with five thin stacks of bills. "See?"

"Thank you."

"If you give me a check, you can take them away."

"That's all right. I just wanted to see them."

"You want to measure them?"

Lucy let herself through the gate. "That's fine. Fine. Thanks."

"When will it be on?"

"Next season," Lucy said. "Sunday night. Movie of the week."

★ ★ ★

Now that she knew what she was looking for, she searched every hiding place in the office: the pictures again, the back of the mirror, the tiny closet, the desk. There was no money, but in the course of her search, she came across the envelope from the morgue and studied the contents of the wallet again. This time she saw the significance of the tiny plastic reading lens, and the pair of bifocals. Trimble was not wearing glasses in any of his pictures; there was another pair of half-glasses in the drawer that he wore for reading, apparently, and yet another pair in his apartment. The plastic lens propped up his vanity by enabling him to read telephone books and race cards without putting on glasses. Lucy slipped on the bifocals from the envelope. They were a good fit on her but she could see nothing through them. She tried on the reading glasses she had found in the desk and they immediately fell off, an inch, at least, too wide, but by holding them on, she found she could read through them quite well. The bifocals, then, were not his. Now a new scenario formed in her head. The glasses had obviously been dropped near David's body by whoever stole the money. Probably David had kept the money in his office, perhaps was even handling it, counting it, that morning, and was interrupted. There was a struggle, a scuffle, the intruder's glasses fell off, and David collapsed on them as the thief took the money and ran. All she had to do was identify the owner.

She put the glasses back and finished her search, her head humming with names. Had MacGovern come by to pick up his half? Nolan? The jockey? Johnny? Or one of Cowan's boys? Determined to do each step thoroughly, she put the office back together and drove out to David's apartment. At the door of his block she nearly turned back to do what she knew she should do, but she was reluctant to abandon Johnny to the police until she was quite sure. What troubled her most about Johnny was the possibility that he had been courting her to find out what she had discovered. If that was so, she would go back to Longborough.

Searching the apartment again was simple, for she had already looked in most of the available hiding places. She took the cushions off the single armchair and prodded every inch. The cracks between the seat and the frame yielded only a paper clip, some coins, and two peppermints. She took the mattress off the bed and marched up and down it in her stockinged feet; it was made

261

of foam rubber and there were no lumps anywhere.

The next morning she remembered to make a copy of the diary on a soft disk and seal it in an envelope, on which she wrote, "To be opened if necessary." This she gave to Tse.

"What's this?"

"Keep it safe. In case."

"In case of what?" He stared at her, then realizing what she meant, he laughed, then quickly got angry. "What the hell are you up to? You think you've found out something, don't you? You think you're going to be killed or something? For Chrissake, stop it. Go to the police." He reached for the phone. "I'll call them."

"What are you going to say?"

He slammed the phone down. "What are you up to?" he shouted.

"I think David might have had a lot of money somewhere, and someone came looking for it and I'm going to find out where it is. That's all I want to say right now."

"I'll tell you something. People do kill each other for money, the kind of people David Trimble knew. You're not going to take any chances like that."

She stared at him, hearing Geoffrey. Geoffrey would have said, "I'm not having you take chances like that." They all think they own you, she thought. And, immediately, seeing the worry on Tse's face, she relented. When Geoffrey said it, he was concerned about himself, out of a fear that his wife would do something to embarrass him for which he would be held responsible. Peter Tse, on the other hand, was simply being protective. He said it because he liked her, wanted to look after her. Still.

"It's just a precaution," she said, very quietly.

"It's a bloody silly precaution and you're a bloody silly woman." His anger remained, the anger of a parent who has pulled back his child from the edge of a cliff. "What are you going to do? Run around and tell all the people who knew David that you're looking for his money? Accuse all these people, one by one?"

"I'm going to do a bit more work first. Make certain of what I think I've learned."

Now Tse was furious. "What the hell are you talking about? What the hell do you think you've found out?"

But Lucy stayed stubborn. She was frightened, of course, but she wanted to be certain of Johnny's involvement. It was becoming another kind of test or trial. "I can't tell you," she said. "I've got very good evidence that David had a large sum of money around and either it's still here or David was robbed."

In the violence of his rage, Tse approached her as if to do her an injury. "Your cousin never had a thousand dollars at one time in the last ten years. He was a bookie's runner who fancied himself; a nothing, a nobody, a fool, an arsehole. He liked to rub elbows with the big boys — look at these pictures — but some of the big boys he knew were big-time scum. I want to know what all this is about."

She had said too much. He wouldn't leave her alone now. "Don't bug me anymore, Peter. I promise you, I'll let you know as soon as I can."

Tse hissed explosively through his teeth and left, slamming the door behind him.

So much for inscrutable, Lucy thought.

The phone rang again, and again.

Chapter 32

The discovery that she was surrounded by swindlers nearly drove the agoraphobic woman out of Lucy's mind, but the appearance of the husband reminded her that it was a very easy hundred and fifty dollars a week he provided. Once more, though, she tried to convince him to try to deal with his wife's problems, but when he cut her off she shrugged and put the money in a drawer. This time, she thought, with Nina; but again Nina was too busy and again begged her to postpone any intervention until she could be there. "It could be like waking a sleep-walker," she said. "It'll certainly be a shock when she finds out she's been looked after."

That night Lucy followed the woman down to Bloor Street, where she turned west, driving slowly, obviously dawdling to look at the Bloor Street scene. They crawled along the curb between Spadina and Bathurst and then turned south, past Honest Ed's, to Queen Street, where they turned east again. Now they were passing Lucy's office, and she was pleasantly surprised to see how lively the street was at night if she ever decided to work late. They made no effort to pass any streetcars until they reached City Hall, where the woman accelerated, scooting across several intersections before settling down to some steady driving.

The Beach, thought Lucy, this is where they say the Beach is. She had heard the name from several people of whom she had enquired about things to do and see in Toronto, and she had promised herself a visit to the area the next time she had Sunday free. Because on Sundays, they said, Queen Street beyond the racetrack was the favorite boulevard of all the Torontonians who did not live in the area, attracting thousands of people who sauntered up one side and back down the other, eating, drinking, crowd-watching, and window-shopping the dozens of small stores that had sprung up to serve this new public.

This wasn't Sunday but something was going on. Much of the traffic turned into a big parking lot near the racetrack, and the people walked back to Queen Street to what was obviously some kind of street music festival. She could hear the music from the parking lot, and as soon as she joined the crowds she saw them, musicians, singly and in pairs, in small groups and large bands, with and without amplification, banging, plucking, blowing, shaking, in every idiom from folk to rock, and with every sound from New Orleans to tin-whistle paddywhackery.

The crowd was so thick it was impossible to see the woman, and Lucy immediately decided not to care. "I'm enjoying this," she thought. "Besides, it must be paradise for an agoraphobic, if that's what she is."

They shuffled from block to block, each one occupied by a different musical group. A streetcar came along, trying to carve a path through the crowd that filled the street; many of the passengers had the worried look of people who have found themselves on the wrong tour, but an extraordinary number were hanging out the windows, taking pictures. After a mile or so she came up to four Peruvians in pot hats, playing pipes of different kinds. One of them began to sing, and by way of chorus jumped up and down, joined, at first, by the other three, still playing, then by some of the crowd, then by some more of the crowd including Lucy. This is what I came to Toronto for, she thought, waiting for the cue to start jumping again. Who cares about a bunch of crooks?

After the Peruvian jump-up music, she slipped into a doorway to look at her feet, which had been stepped on several times, then decided to go the rest of the way by streetcar. She bought an ice cream cone and fought her way onto the next car. A small Chinese girl gave up her seat, and Lucy rode happily along for the twenty minutes it took to get back to the parking lot.

Her only dilemma, as she turned the car west on Bloor again, was how much to charge her client. Probably nothing, because losing the woman must invalidate the agreement. And then she saw her car again, fifty yards behind, and Lucy dawdled in the curb lane until the woman passed her and she got back on her tail. A hundred and fifty. Who could say her nay?

The next day, since nothing could happen about the diary until she made it happen, Lucy decided to clean up the Longborough identification before she did any more. She was very much aware that she was postponing the inevitable by keeping busy, but she couldn't face the immediate destruction of the dream she had taken away with her from Johnny's farm. She wanted to postpone that decision for as long as possible.

She also wanted to know if her house was still standing. Although the answering machine was programmed to offer her Toronto number, she had not yet heard from The

Trog, which had provided a further space to test her feelings about him. She had not missed him at all, but that might only be because life in Toronto had been so full. And she wanted to find out how she felt about Longborough itself, now that she might have to return. Then, too, Jack Brighton had been very relaxed about the assignment, but he would surely require a response soon. She was still in business; she had to forget about Johnny Comstock and finish her other assignments.

As she drove into Longborough that morning she felt immediately the distance she had traveled in the last few weeks. Downtown Longborough is charmless: A few decaying department stores survive at the main intersections, but most of the life has been sucked out of the center and spewed up onto a strip of development near the main highway, a strip consisting mainly of outlets of every fast-food chain in North America, plus a few motels. There is no refurbished nineteenth-century main street with the original (restored) hotel, and the first (1812) grain-and-feed store now converted into an organic foods store. Longborough's downtown consists of several blocks of utilitarian buildings interspersed with vacant lots. It supplies the day-to-day

269

needs of its citizens but offers nothing in the way of a piazza in which to meet and stroll and restore the spirit. For the new Lucy, compared to the corner of Queen and Spadina, it was nowhere.

There was no message in her mailbox from The Trog, for which she felt a mild relief. Perhaps, like her, he had simply moved on. But it was nice to be in the house again, to remember what therapy it had once provided, for Longborough improves immediately as you move away from the center, and though Lucy's house was close to downtown it stood on a street of solidly built houses, each decently surrounded with grass, a street lined with big, peaceful trees. And beyond the street, a drive of half an hour through the rolling countryside led to the Kawarthas, the lake country that many Torontonians find beautiful enough to be worth a two-to-three-hour drive every weekend to their summer cottages.

It took only an hour of searching through land titles to confirm that the farm now owned by Nora Denton was owned in 1940 by Harold Potter, and instinct told Lucy to leave it there for the moment. She had no doubt that Harold Potter was Brian Potter's uncle, and that his daughter, Nora

Denton, was Brian Potter's cousin and now his sole heir, but to get the final document would mean alerting the Dentons. She could do that last. In the meantime she had another name to check. The news about Brian Potter's death had been brought to the Dentons originally by a Mrs. Tibbles, and Lucy thought she should confirm the original story through this connection if she could. She learned from the secretary of the Longborough Historical Society that the Tibbleses had been one of Longborough's leading families before the last war. They were Longborough's "old money," the family fortune having its roots in buying land cheap and selling it dear to immigrants in the middle of the nineteenth century, and after that its tentacles reached into lumber, flour, meat, and construction. Sometime in the sixties the family moved to Toronto, much to the regret of Longborough, because the Tibbleses had now been rich enough for long enough to have developed a philanthropic streak and regularly donated to a number of worthy causes. But much of the business in Longborough stayed in the family's hands. Old Mr. Tibbles was dead, but his wife was still alive, and her son still looked after the family's interests from Toronto.

Back in Toronto, Lucy reported to Jack Brighton, telephoned the only Tibbles with a Rosedale number, and got an appointment with Mrs. Tibbles that afternoon.

Alice Tibbles lived with a cousin in a house on Roxborough that seemed too big for two old ladies.

"At least, everyone seems to think so, but I've lived here for thirty years, and it's just big enough so that my grandchildren and their children can stay overnight when they come to town, and I can still walk everywhere, including to the liquor store."

She was a small, soft woman whose perfume carried across the room. She had been pretty in a chocolate-box way once and still managed her roundness daintily, down to the little bows on her shoes. Her voice was soft and breathy, like Eve in the garden, but it seemed possible that she was sometimes giving her words a spin. Her remark about the liquor store, for instance, given her age and the probability, growing up where she did, of a mildly prohibitionist background, could be read as a criticism of the kind of thing other people would be grateful for, or as indicating a wish to show what a wicked old lady she was, or as a statement of fact. It was not possible to be sure. She seemed like an eighty-year-old, nicely brought up Marilyn Monroe.

Her cousin, equally ancient, but still being addressed by her nursery diminutive of "Fluffy," said, "We are each other's alarm system. If I weren't here, Alice would have to wear a beeper around her neck in case she needed help, as I would."

Mrs. Tibbles turned her blue eyes full on her cousin until she was sure she had finished. "Yes," she breathed. "Awful."

Fluffy said, "I'll make some tea."

"Henry will be here soon," Alice said. She turned to Lucy. "My son," she explained.

Both ladies were perfectly mobile, and by sitting in hard chairs had minimal difficulty getting up and down. Fluffy, in fact, still managed a little spring as she rose.

When she had disappeared, Lucy raised the topic of the Dentons.

"Tell me again what it is you are doing," Mrs. Tibbles said.

Lucy explained that she was a private detective hired by an English law firm to enquire into the whereabouts of Brian Potter.

"Oh, my. A detective."

Again Lucy could not tell if the wonder in her tone was real or mocking.

Mrs. Tibbles said, "He died, you know, in Quebec. He got ill on the train coming from Halifax, and he died in hospital."

"Do you remember the name of the hospital?"

"Of course. Trois-Rivières."

Lucy had now done everything she could. No doubt a copy of the death certificate could be procured from Trois-Rivières. Fluffy brought in tea and poured for everyone, and then, making conversation, Lucy asked, "Were you the official Longborough person for looking after these evacuees when they arrived?"

"Yes." She gave the word a roundness and emphasis as if she had selected it from a hundred alternatives. "But that wasn't why I went to the Dentons' farm. I think I felt sorry for them, and wanted to say so."

"What happened to Brian's other things? There was a list of enclosures, a watch, his wallet, things like that."

"I'm sure I don't know. Perhaps they never left the hospital. All I got was a letter."

"Made out by the hospital?"

"Yes. They hadn't been able to find Brian's mother, you see, so they asked me to find the relative he was going to."

"Why you? Why did they approach you?"

"They had tried to get to the Potters directly, but for some reason the postmaster in Longborough sent it back, so they tried me. My son was on the ship, you see, and a sort of friend of Brian's. He went to the hospital to help them interpret, because he'd been to France for his holidays, and Brian couldn't speak any French. I got a telegram saying that Henry would be on the next day's train. Brian died very quickly. I did know who the Potters were, of course, so they asked me. Yes. That's how it was."

Lucy said, "Could your son confirm the death?"

"Oh, he will. He's coming by soon. You can talk to him. I've warned him you will be here."

Now they had run out of business until the son arrived. Mrs. Tibbles said, "Tell us about your work, Mrs. Brenner. Is it very dangerous?" Again she looked with wide blue eyes at Fluffy, and again she might simply have been politely including Fluffy in the conversation, or signaling to her cousin that she was about to send Lucy up. The little smile would have been equally suitable for both.

But within a few sentences they were talking not about Lucy's work, but about Longborough, comparing the Longborough Lucy had found when she fled Kingston with the one that Alice and Fluffy had left behind. "We still have a cottage on Stony Lake,"

Alice said, "but I haven't been up for several years."

At six there was the noise of someone coming in, and Fluffy put the tea tray together. "You won't need me," she said, and left.

Standing in the doorway, waiting to be introduced, was a lightly built man of about sixty with fair hair turning gray and a pleasant expression that seemed to have survived from his boyhood.

"My son, Henry," Mrs. Tibbles said. "Mrs. Brenner, the detective."

He shook hands with Lucy, kissed his mother, and moved to the sideboard. "Let me get us a drink."

Lucy thought of saying no, but for no good reason, and when Mrs. Tibbles said, "It *is* six o'clock," accepted that as a good reason for saying yes.

"Mother drinks gin, but I want Scotch," Henry said. "What about you?"

Lucy said, "What I would really like is a rye and ginger."

"I'll join you," Tibbles said promptly. "Haven't had a drink of rye for years."

Smooth, thought Lucy.

"I was raised on it," Mrs. Tibbles said. "But the bubbles give me heartburn now."

Don't overdo it, Lucy thought. But however much she held the remark up to the light she could find nothing in it but a desire to make her feel comfortable, and she relaxed.

When everyone had a drink, Tibbles said, "Mother tells me you want to know about Brian Potter."

"I think I know all I need now, thanks. You were with him."

"We struck up a bit of a friendship, right from the train journey going up to Liverpool from London, and on the ship. It was a shock when he died. Have you ever seen anyone die of meningitis?"

Lucy shook her head.

"I imagine they can relieve it now, the pain, I mean, with drugs, but they didn't seem able to then."

"Where is he buried?"

"In the Protestant cemetery at Trois-Rivières. I went back once, a long time after, to see the grave and arrange a headstone."

"It's good of you to see me, and there's no need to prolong this. It must have been a sad shock to his uncle."

Mrs. Tibbles said, "I thought so, that's why I went to see him when the letter came. Have you seen the farm? Oh, yes, you said so."

There was a long silence, then Lucy said,

"Have you seen the farm since? Lately?"

"A month ago. Henry drove me to Longborough to see an old friend and we came home past the Denton place."

"How did it look to you?"

"About the same as it looked in 1940."

Lucy had a desire to share with Alice her disgust at the Dentons' lifestyle but she did not know if such talk would be welcome, so she thanked them both again, swallowed her rye, and made to leave. Before she could, however, Tibbles had a fresh drink for her. "You owe us a story," he said, smiling. "Who wants to know about Brian at this date? Not his mother, surely. She abandoned him fifty years ago."

"Sent him to Canada, you mean?"

"Abandoned him," Tibbles said firmly. "And told him so. A little chat in the railway station in London, when she told him to try and be a good boy and make a life with his uncle because she was going to have to go away and might not be there after the war. Abandoned him."

"Well, it's because of her that I'm here. She died recently, and made some provision for Brian in her will." Lucy swigged her drink. "Left him the lot."

"Very much?" Tibbles asked.

"I don't know."

278

"What a pity," Alice breathed. "What happens now?"

"It goes to the nearest relatives, I guess."

"But they couldn't find any other relatives when they wanted to send the letter in 1940, except the Potters, of course."

"So it goes to Nora Denton, I guess."

"Oh, my."

Lucy stood up. "Would you mind giving me a written account of Brian's death?" she asked.

"I'll send it to your office," Henry said.

Chapter 33

"So there you are, Jack. Fax those English lawyers that a signed witness's statement is forthcoming, and that Nora Denton was his cousin. That should do it."

Three days later, before Tibbles's statement arrived, Brighton showed Lucy a fax saying that the name of the hospital had enabled the English lawyers to get a death certificate, and now they were sure the courts would accept Nora Denton as the rightful heir.

At the same time, still pushing Johnny out of her mind, and curious to know if anything had been made of this sad story at the time, Lucy drove back to Longborough and looked through the files of the *Examiner* for 1940 and came across the story, complete with a picture of the dead boy, a picture that bothered her so much that with Jack Brighton's consent, after she had explained the problem, she faxed the English lawyers to see if Mrs. Potter still had a picture of her son when she died. She got back a copy of a snapshot taken during the first year of the war. Now, for the first time since she had read Trimble's diary, she had something that took up all her attention.

She knew how casually the *Examiner* might have been edited in 1940, how easy it still was for even Canada's national newspaper to put the wrong name on a picture, and she considered what she should do. She remembered Henry Tibbles saying he had been at school in England, and the name of the school, Clanfield, and she composed a query to a detective agency in London, England, asking about Tibbles and requesting any pictures taken around 1940, and persuaded the *Examiner* to make her a copy of the newspaper picture of Brian Potter to send with it. Before she sent it off, she showed the letter to Jack Brighton.

He said, "It'd be quicker to go yourself."

"To England?"

"Sure. You have anything else on? There's a guy named Comstock trying to track you down, by the way. What's that all about?"

"He's trying to sell me a horse. Don't tell him anything. How long will it take me to go to England and back? A week?"

"You could go tonight, get there in the morning, go down to this village, find out what you want to know, and catch the plane back tomorrow afternoon. Or stay overnight.

Come back on Wednesday."

The idea made her gulp, but Brighton was looking at her as he had the first day when he had offered her the Longborough job, daring her, and it was a perfect way of dwelling less on her misery. "I'll stay the night," she said. "Do a little shopping at Harrods. Come back in time to follow Mrs. Lindberg."

"Attagirl."

"But I thought you had to book months in advance, or pay thousands of dollars."

"There are ways." Brighton held up a finger and pulled out the telephone book. He dialed a number, then said, "I'm looking for a ticket to London any plane tonight, come back any plane on Wednesday. Family emergency. Funeral. Sure." He tucked the phone under his ear, and said to Lucy, "What are you going to do when you find out that the paper got some pictures mixed up? No big deal."

But Lucy had had time to think. She smiled. "That is not going to happen."

He held up a hand, cutting her off. "Hello, yeah. That's good. Great. She'll be there. Yeah. I'll let you speak to her."

He handed over the phone. "They want your Visa number."

When she had finished, Brighton said,

"Do me a favor? Bring me back some of those, like, chocolate walnut whorls. I think they're Rowntree's. My dad used to bring them back for us when we were kids. You can't get them here."

Lucy was about to say that she was sure she had seen them on sale in Toronto, then stopped herself. Who knew what Jack's father might have been up to when he said he was going abroad? "I'll scour London," she said.

In the next six hours, Lucy planned and prepared a trip to England, something that she would have allocated six months to under ordinary Longborough circumstances.

At first, when she listed what she had to do to be ready, she saw that the expedition was impossible, and then, slowly, she delisted everything inessential and asked Nina about the rest. As she had suspected, Nina had all the answers.

"Get some money out of the machine and change a hundred dollars at the airport. Take some more to change there. How much? A day? Two hundred. Pay for your hotel and everything else with your card. Put together the outfit you want to wear in England; pack it; wear slacks and a sweater and sneakers on the plane; change in the washroom at Heathrow; take a book you've already read, an old favorite, to read on the plane. That's it. Have a good time."

Happily, Lucy had a valid passport, continually renewed since her only trip abroad, to Bermuda, before she was married. It, along with her heavy raincoat, was in Longborough.

The round-trip to Longborough took four hours, and when she got back to Toronto she had time only to put a notice on her door, saying when she would be back, and buy some underwear before she had to leave for the airport.

Lucy had only a vague notion of what flying was like these days. She was astonished at the lack of fuss, and the absence of lineups, and delighted on the plane to find that the stewardess in charge of her section was older than she was, and called her "dear," as if Lucy were already in England. She had a martini, and two glasses of red wine with her dinner, which, contrary to what everyone had always said, she found tasty and ingeniously laid out, and then she had a B and B afterward. On land she knew she would have felt slightly skunked, and she did not know that the altitude was supposed to intensify the effect of the alcohol: Her head seemed clear as a bell, so much so that she made no attempt to sleep, and watched the movie, a Harrison Ford adventure. After that she looked at her book for a while, and then the sky lightened and the kindly old stewardess brought her breakfast, which consisted of a bran muffin, a tiny croissant, and a sticky bun, all very cold, a little foil-covered beaker of orange juice, and tea. "Not very brilliant, love," the stewardess said about the breakfast, "but it'll hold you until you get on dry land." Lucy left the plane feeling that she had spent eight hours in a cinema where an extravagantly colored movie played on a wraparound screen.

After customs, Lucy learned from the British Rail desk that she should take the bus to Reading and the train to Oxford. From there she would be able to get a bus to Whitney and change there, probably, for Clanfield. "Can't be sure," the clerk said. "These local services aren't too brilliant sometimes, but I think that's your best bet."

Lucy went out to wait under the gray sky for the bus to Reading, due in twenty minutes. It was now three o'clock in the morning, Toronto time, and she dozed gently, leaning against the signpost, like a horse.

At Reading, the driver shook her awake.

"Don't want to go back to Heathrow, do we?" he asked. "Where are you going? Oxford? Through that door and across to the platform on the far side. Oh no, they've changed it. No Entry. That's brilliant, isn't it? Better ask inside."

"Brilliant," used pejoratively, seemed to be the adjective of choice in England that year.

She asked just in time to get to the right platform as an Oxford train pulled in. Seated, she had the clever idea of enquiring loudly, of anyone who cared to be looking, if this was the Oxford train. Four other passengers agreed that it was, and she got another twenty minutes' sleep before they shook her awake at Oxford.

At Oxford, instead of the cold drizzle that she hoped for to freshen her up, the air was thick and used-up, and by the time she found the right bus at Gloucester Green her feet weren't lifting high enough to get up the steps. "Whitney," she said to the driver, sitting across from him, and fell into a deep sleep.

She woke up to find the bus stopped, all eyes upon her, and the driver saying, "If she were a few years younger I'd've said drugs, but I think she's just had a few." Seeing her eyes open, he shouted "Whitney" at her and grinned around the bus as if Lucy were a foreigner.

Eventually, in Clanfield, Lucy walked across to The Plough and ordered a ham sandwich and coffee, took them into the lounge, and sank with them into the most comfortable armchair she had ever experienced in her whole life. The landlord woke her up at two, and she drank another cup of coffee and asked directions to the school. "Didn't anyone tell you it's ten miles from here?" he asked, not unkindly.

"I didn't know anyone to ask."

He shook his head. "Brilliant," he said. "You stay there for a few minutes. I'll call you a taxi to take you to the school. All right? What're you up to, then? Visiting your grandson, are you?"

Lucy went into the lavatory and tried to recover her own image from the ancient gray face that stared back at her. In the end she settled for a wash and the look of someone, not much older than she, who had led a very hard life.

The taxi driver dropped her at the gate — "Bit difficult turning round inside," he said — and she tottered up the drive to the front door, where a man in overalls listened to her story and directed her to the office of the school secretary. Here, a small, fat woman with a sarcastic face and an accent so exquisite that Lucy thought she was doing it for effect — all of her words were manufactured in a tiny space behind her teeth and ejected from between nearly closed lips — proved to be very willing to investigate Lucy's problem. Later, Lucy suspected that she looked as if she were at the end of a lifelong quest, conducted without food, water, or sleep, and that must have helped to arouse sympathy, or simply moved people to respond quickly to get her off the premises before she needed medical assistance.

"A family connection, is it? A distant cousin, you think? Tibbles? About 1940?" It took no time at all. The secretary, Miss Dunn, turned to a highly polished oak cabinet behind her, like an old library index, pulled out a drawer, and flicked her thumb through it, shaking her head. "I would have remembered him from other searches," she said. "No. No boy named Tibbles has ever been enrolled at Clanfield. You can trust this file, Mrs. Brenner. Is there anything else I can do for you? You *have* come a long way."

Lucy opened her purse and pulled out a copy of the picture in the Longborough *Examiner*. "Can you tell me if this boy ever went to Clanfield? About 1940?"

"The caption says he is Brian Potter," the

secretary pointed out. Before Lucy could stop her she had flicked through her file again. "No. No Brian Potter, either. Rotten luck."

"That caption's wrong."

Miss Dunn thought about this. "Then it might be more difficult. I mean, unless you *knew* him, you could easily compare him to all the faces in the group pictures and not see any resemblance, or, just as likely, see a resemblance to half a dozen boys. It's not a very good picture, is it, Mrs. Brenner? Mrs. Brenner!"

Lucy opened her eyes. "I was thinking," she said.

"Yes. Could you leave the picture with me? There's an old lady in the village who used to help with the washing, and she claims she remembers every boy who was ever at the school. I'll ask her."

"Would you? Yes. I've got an extra copy."

"Your address?"

Lucy produced one of the cards that Jack Brighton had supplied her with.

"I thought you said you were a distant relative?"

Lucy said, "You misheard. I'm enquiring *on behalf* of a distant relative. Sorry."

"I see. Well, I'll ask Mrs. Perry, anyway."

The taxi took her back to The Plough to

wait for her bus. It was five o'clock and Lucy sat on the bench outside the inn, planning how best to use her time. Her list of possible outings the day before had included Harrods, a walk round Oxford, and going to a play in London. A figure appeared in front of her, the host of The Plough.

"Find your grandson?"

"Yes, thank you."

"Now what?"

"I'm waiting for a bus to Whitney."

"Another hour and a half, I'm afraid."

Lucy gave up. "Brilliant," she said. She looked across at the obviously well-managed inn. "Do you rent rooms?" she asked.

"I think we could find you one." He picked up her little bag. "Will you want dinner?"

"Not yet. But eventually. I think I'll take a little nap. Could you call me at seven, say?"

So she napped until seven, ate a good dinner, sat in the lounge with her Agatha Christie for half an hour afterward, then went back to bed and slept for ten hours. In the morning she traveled back to Heathrow, promising the passing scenery that she would be back.

Chapter 34

In Toronto, she reported to Jack Brighton the next morning. He had a message for her already, a fax from Miss Dunn. Old Mrs. Perry had positively identified the picture in the Longborough *Examiner* as one J. (Jim) Lacey, a Clanfield boy who had gone out to Canada in 1940, after his parents were killed in the blitz.

"What does that tell you?" Brighton asked.

"I'm not sure, but I think I have to have a chat with Mrs. Tibbles. There's no rush. I want to work it out first."

The procrastination was almost over, but there was one more lead to follow before she made up her mind that there was no other explanation. Lucy talked next to Cowan, the bookmaker. As far as she knew, Cowan had simply been involved in settling a bet of fifty thousand dollars, but there was the possibility that having satisfied some kind of gambler's code by paying off the bet, Cowan had then decided to recover the money. In which case, there might be some risk in approaching him, but it had to be done.

She found him at home in the Ulysses Diner. After he had allowed her to sit down and sent the protective waiter away, Lucy started right in. "I've come across my cousin's diary," she said. "There was a bet. On a race on the seventh of June. A horse called Sly Peek won at ten to one. My cousin had five thousand on."

"Trimble bet five thousand?" He spoke each word softly, wonderingly, giving each the same emphasis, as though reciting numbers. "Not with me."

"The diary says so. And it says you paid off."

Cowan leaned forward, interested. "Does it really?"

"Yes, it does. But the money has disappeared."

"I'm not surprised." Cowan giggled briefly.

"Why would you be? You were the only one who knew he actually had it."

Cowan examined his fingernails. Not having protested immediately, he could now take his own time. "May I have it all again?" he asked. "Just to be sure I know what I've done."

Only slightly unnerved by Cowan's calm, Lucy went through the scam again.

"So therefore I took it back?" Cowan asked.

"That's what I think."

"I wouldn't do that."

"You might, if you found out that the race was fixed."

"Did I find that out?"

"The diary doesn't say so. But I think you might have realized."

Cowan nodded to the waiter who was watching by the bar, and received another cup of coffee. "Mrs. Brenner, how was the race fixed?"

Lucy drew out the photocopy of the race result and handed it to him. "The favorite was Desk Lamp. According to the diary, my cousin was in a conspiracy to make sure Desk Lamp won, but David and, I think, Johnny Comstock double-crossed the others and made sure Sly Peek won. David had bet five thousand on Sly Peek."

"With me?"

Lucy nodded. She consulted her copy of the diary. "You didn't lay it off because you learned that the trainer of Sly Peek was betting on Desk Lamp, so you thought David was being conned. But David was doing the conning."

"And how did they fix the race?" Cowan's attitude was that of a man hearing marvels.

"Drugs. David got hold of some drugs that would not show up in tests, one to slow down Sly Peek, the other to speed up Desk Lamp."

"How many people were involved? David would need help."

"MacGovern, David, Johnny Comstock, and someone called Nolan."

"Ah, Nolan," Cowan said, as if there was some sense emerging.

"They all thought they were part of a swindle to make Desk Lamp win, but David switched the drugs, double-crossing everybody, including you because of what you thought he was up to. But you paid up."

"Honor among thieves, eh?" Cowan took a bullet-shaped white plastic cylinder from an inside pocket and jammed it in a nostril, inhaling deeply. He turned to a blank page in his notebook. "I want to get this all down," he said. "I may write my own memoirs some day."

"Mr. Cowan, I don't know what you find to enjoy in all this, but don't pretend you don't know all about it. The bet, I mean."

Cowan ignored this. "How did the double-cross work? Tell me again. Slow, so I can get it down."

Lucy went through it once more.

"I see. And I paid up? And you think I may have tried to get my money back."

"Probably, yes. After David died. You were the only one who knew he had it."

Cowan looked at his notes and at the printout of the race. "I have to go back to work," he said. "But this bears thinking about. Would you do me a favor? Would you trust me? There's something here I don't quite understand. I wish you'd leave it with me for a day or two."

Lucy found his attitude baffling. He was utterly unperturbed, just interested. And why should she trust him? There was no way of knowing what he planned to do. He still seemed like a retired chicken farmer with nice manners, but she was more or less frightened of the idea of him. But then she thought that no one would dare touch her. "You remember what I said the other day," she said. "That a copy . . ."

"Yes, yes, yes. You have deposited a copy of this diary with your lawyer to be opened if anything happens to you. Never fear. Wally Buncombe, was it?"

"How did you know?"

"Wally looks after a lot of people round Woodbine."

"I'm going to tackle Johnny Comstock."

"Not yet. Let's surprise him."

"That's what I want to do. He surprised me enough."

Cowan looked at her thoughtfully. "I see. When will you surprise him?"

"He's got a horse running next Wednesday."

"That'll give me time."

Whatever Cowan's plan was, he was not going to disclose it to her, but she could see little risk in waiting. "I don't want anyone hurt," she said.

"Never fear, Mrs. Brenner. Never fear."

And there was the detail that she hadn't told anyone, which gave her an idea for developing an ace up her sleeve. The glasses. Back in her office, she called Jack Brighton. "There's something I want to talk to you about. Do you mind?"

"I told you, if you're going to pick my brains, it'll cost you."

"Take it off my finder's fee."

In Brighton's office she produced the glasses, and found that she had to tell Brighton some of the story.

"You think he might have been frightened by someone who came to collect a bet, had a heart attack, collapsed, and this other guy took the money and ran, dropping his glasses on the way? How much time is unaccounted for before that travel agent noticed him on the floor?"

"Not long. Hardly any time, really. But enough."

"All right, I'll find out if I can track down the owner of these specs. I wouldn't think so."

"Do you have a magnifying glass?"

"Well, yeah." Brighton grinned and blushed. "I've never used it before." He opened a drawer and retrieved a large black-rimmed lens, then closed the blinds. "Slip the catch on that door, would you. I feel like a horse's ass with this thing. Someone might walk in. So what am I looking for?"

"Inside the earpiece. There's a whole series of numbers and letters. They must be some kind of identification."

Brighton looked through his glass, still with the stance of a man who does not want to make a fool of himself. "Right," he said. "You're right. There they are. Okay. I'll call you. What now?"

"I promised everyone I would wait two days."

"That's probably best. I should have the answer to this by then."

Chapter 35

There were no more calls from Johnny, and The Trog had stayed away. The next day she wrapped up the case of the Longborough heir, pulled back to it by a phone message, a request by Mrs. Tibbles to call. Lucy telephoned and Fluffy said that by "call" Alice meant in person, and they would wait for her.

Before she left, Lucy thought through the case again. There seemed now to be three boys: Tibbles, Potter, and Lacey. Potter was dead, Tibbles was in Toronto, so where was Lacey? And why was Lacey identified in the *Examiner* as the dead Potter? If, somehow, Potter was not dead, but another boy had been so identified, a boy named Lacey, then where was Potter? Because the legacy was his, and Lucy was determined to keep the Dentons' hands off it until she was sure. She was going to have to trace these three boys through the passenger lists, the Red Cross lists, everywhere they might have been recorded in their transatlantic journey. She felt the need of Brighton's help, but there was no time before she had to leave to see Mrs. Tibbles.

When they were settled in the living room, once more with tea, Alice said, "You've been very busy, Mrs. Brenner. You're very good at your work, aren't you?"

"I've done my job. Or rather, I'm doing it. I don't think I've finished yet."

"What haven't you figured out yet?" Mrs. Tibbles breathed interestedly, as if sharing with Lucy a mutual crossword problem.

"Quite a lot, but I do have a place to start. The last time I was here your son said that he had been at school in England, at a place called Clanfield. There is no record of a boy named Tibbles ever having gone to that school."

Mrs. Tibbles nodded. "Anything else?"

"There is a picture of someone identified as Brian Potter in the Longborough *Examiner* accompanying the story of his death. It's not Brian Potter. It's a boy named Lacey. A boy who did go to Clanfield."

"What did you plan to do next? Hello, Henry," she said to her son, who had just arrived and sat down next to his mother.

Lucy said, "In the first place I was hired to find Brian Potter, and then when I found he was dead, to establish that Nora Denton is his cousin, because she apparently stands to get some money. Now, I'd like to know what happened on that train, and perhaps that ship, and maybe the Dentons' farm. I suppose I want to make sure that Nora Denton doesn't get the money until I am certain Brian Potter is dead, and how he died."

"So what are you going to do?"

Now Lucy looked long and hard at Henry Tibbles. "First, I'm going to look at the records in Longborough going back to about 1930 to see who was born at that time. Then I'm going to try to find out what happened to the boy Lacey who was sent to Canada in 1940, at the same time as Brian Potter and your son."

Tibbles leaned forward in his chair and squeezed his hands together, looking at his feet. His mother watched him, waiting for a signal. Tibbles looked at Lucy then, and said, "Mrs. Brenner. I suppose I ought to start by asking if you could let sleeping dogs lie, or some such. First of all, you aren't going to find some terrible dark secret behind this. No one has killed anyone. No ten-year-old that you don't know about lies in a grave in the Dentons' back forty. But you won't take my word for this, will you?"

"I can't, can I?"

The Tibbleses seemed at a loss, as if they needed a "time-out" before they said anything else. Lucy said, "How did you know I was still working on the case?"

Mrs. Tibbles came close to putting an edge on her voice. "My family has friends, still, at Clanfield, Mrs. Brenner, and in Longborough in the municipal offices as well as the newspaper office. When you make enquiries about something touching me, they naturally tell me. And there are other detectives in Toronto."

Lucy nodded. A lesson learned. "Can you save me some trouble, then? If I go to the records of births in Longborough around 1930, what will I find?"

"I've been thinking," Tibbles said. "You're not working for anyone at the moment. You've satisfied the queries you had from England. This latest business you're doing on your own behalf. How about working for us? We'll pay a retainer. Say five thousand dollars." He glanced at his mother, who nodded.

"What would I do?"

"Nothing."

She shook her head. "I have a feeling that I'm going to look silly before I leave here, but I want to know."

"What?"

"Who was the boy Lacey, and where is he now?"

Again the Tibbleses exchanged looks, and Mrs. Tibbles with a tiny nod released her son to speak.

"I thought it might come to this, so I'll answer your question, and then, if you don't mind, tell you a story. The boy Lacey is lying in a cemetery in Trois-Rivières."

"And you are Brian Potter," Lucy said quickly, only because she wanted credit for having discovered this before he told her.

"How did you know?" Mrs. Tibbles's voice seemed fainter than ever.

Lucy dug in her purse and produced the photograph the English lawyer had sent her.

"Where did you get this?"

Lucy explained, then realized what the question meant. "You have one, don't you?"

"Yes. He's instantly recognizable, of course." She looked up at Henry, smiling.

"So I am Brian Potter, and the boy Lacey is in the cemetery at Trois-Rivières. As for the boy Tibbles, he never existed, except in me. Shall I start at the beginning?"

"Yes, please."

"Well, then, in 1940 a ten-year-old boy, Brian Potter, was put on a train to Liverpool by his mother. At Liverpool he was to embark on a ship, the *Cumbria*, to Canada, there to join his uncle, also named Potter. He was put in the charge of a Red Cross lady and his mother disappeared. Quite literally. You see, while we were waiting in the train, the news came that the ship would be delayed and we should return four days later. There were three or four children not accompanied by their parents, but in their case the parents were waiting on the platform to wave them off. I was the only one whose parent had disappeared. We had been staying in a hotel in Bloomsbury for the week previously, but when they checked it my mother had never returned. I never saw her again.

"I wasn't surprised. It made sense of a long talk my mother gave me just before she took me to the station, about how I had to be a brave little man and learn to stand on my own two feet because she was not sure what was going to happen to her at this point. In other words, she was abandoning me. I was illegitimate, and a nuisance, and when the war came along, then the opportunity to have a good time — I suppose she was about thirty — was irresistible and she figured out a way to get rid of me. I saw a letter from my uncle in Longborough saying that she could send me over if she liked but to make sure and tell me that it was going to be hard work and no mistake about it, and if I brought any English airs and graces with me they'd soon be knocked out of me. Even at ten I knew what that meant.

"So a kind lady looked after me until the train left and I duly embarked for Canada. I've never forgotten that train: the tiny orange lights because of the blackout, the seats covered in a sort of carpet material, and the window that let down with a huge strap. I rather enjoyed the journey. There were four or five of us traveling alone, and I soon joined up with one about my own age, and we stayed together all the way across."

"The boy Lacey."

"Right. Jim Lacey. He was a wonderful pal, never at a loss for something to do, tougher than me — I suppose the boarding school did that — and imaginative, I suppose you'd have to call it. We played some terrific games that he just made up. One reason why Lacey and I teamed up was we found out from our labels on the train that we were both going to Longborough, Ontario. We didn't have a chaperone after Montreal. The conductor was supposed to look after us, but when Jim got sick, the conductor panicked and called for an ambulance at Trois-Rivières. Well, not panicked, exactly, that's not fair, because Jim was very ill, and he died next day. I went with him to the hospital because someone insisted — I was the only one who knew him. When he died, they took me back to the railway station and I caught the next day's train.

"I'm telling you all this because without it the next bit might seem unlikely. I overheard someone saying he wouldn't recover so I switched identities as we waited for the ambulance at Trois-Rivières. By now I knew all about him, and about this nice aunt who was looking forward to keeping him safe — he'd shown me her letters — and his destiny was in stark contrast to mine, so I switched. I knew she'd never seen Lacey, and I had all the documents and family stories to back me up, so it was easy, I thought. I fooled her completely, I thought." He looked at his mother.

Lucy turned to Mrs. Tibbles. "Did he? It sounds unlikely."

"Of course not." She gave a small chuckle. "What he did was give me time to think. You see, I was in a very disturbed state myself. I had some news for my nephew — since he had left England, his parents had been killed in an air raid and I was now his closest relative — his father had quarreled with his own family — and I didn't know how I could tell him. Then this strange child was foisted on me as Jim Lacey, looking nothing like the picture I had of him, and I heard the story of how Brian Potter, his friend, had died on the journey. I thought the child demented, or shell-shocked, but he kept calling me Auntie, so I thought I'd take him home and talk to a doctor. The next day I got my husband to drive me out to the Dentons' farm, and what I saw there made me very thoughtful. I began to suspect that Jim was not in shock at all, but behaving very rationally indeed. So I went home and talked to Jim until he broke down. It didn't take long — and confessed that he was Brian Potter, and he told me what had happened to Jim. And then I thought, why not? If I let the Dentons have this boy, he will probably become a farm slave — have you ever read the stories of what happened to some of the Barnardo children who were sent out to Canadian farms? — so I thought, who can say us nay, and that was that. I didn't seem to be having any luck having children of my own. When Jim's parents were officially pronounced dead, I applied to adopt him, and so Henry Tibbles was born. Tell me what I've done wrong."

Lucy was silent. Then, "You have all of the Potter boy's identification?"

"Yes. Now tell me what you are going to do?"

"I guess I have some kind of duty to report to the English lawyers that Brian Potter is still alive."

"That damned woman abandons him — before I adopted him I did have someone like you in England search for her but she'd covered her tracks well — and then clears her conscience on her deathbed by opening all this mess up."

"Your son should inherit the money. I don't know how much it is."

"I do. My lawyers enquired. Forty thousand dollars. He doesn't need it."

"Then it goes to the Dentons."

"Yes, that is an objection, all right. Denton will drink it up in three months, but it's a price that's worth paying. On the other hand, if you do go ahead, then there will be a giant embarrassing fuss in the newspapers, Henry will be accused of having committed some kind of crime when he was ten, and I at having connived in it, and Denton won't believe it so he'll insist on having Jim Lacey's body dug up or something equally horrible. Leave it alone. That's why we asked you here. I wanted to stop you making the fatal enquiry that would put anyone else on the track of the story."

"Surely your son's adoption isn't secret?"

"Of course not. It's private, though. Fluffy, a few old friends, and they've no doubt told their children, so most of the people in my world know that at some point Henry was adopted. They also think he was my nephew before I adopted him, as the authorities do. You know different, and I'd like you to forget it."

"All right."

Both Tibbles looked at her steadily.

"All right. Giving Denton forty thousand dollars goes against the grain, though."

"Call it ransom. Now let's have a drink. I feel a bit wobbly."

"You realize that what I did someone else could do? The records are there for anyone to search."

"What you did was awfully clever, and I don't think anyone else could have done it, but just in case, I've taken care that no one else will see the picture in that newspaper's files. The newspaper is still in the family."

Ten minutes later, Lucy left, knowing what she had to do for Mrs. Denton.

Chapter 36

But first, the other world she had been keeping at bay demanded a hearing. On the day before Johnny's next horse ran, she got a call from Nina, asking her to meet in the travel agent's office in an hour. It was, Nina said, extremely important.

An hour later she crossed the street and trotted up the stairs into Nina's office. There, seated in the client's chair, was Johnny Comstock.

Lucy said, "I don't want to talk to you," and turned to leave, stumbling over a chair, but Nina sprang up and took her arm, leading her to her own chair, opposite Johnny. "Listen," she said.

Lucy sat down, avoiding Johnny's eye, concentrating on looking at her own office across the street.

Johnny said, "I hear you're making enquiries. May I know what about?" It was clear from his stillness, and from the lack of expression on his face, that he knew what she had discovered. Cowan, she thought. But why would Cowan talk to a man who had swindled him out of fifty thousand dollars?

Lucy had prepared her speech. "You know what I've found out. I ought to go to the police, but I've decided that the only person who really suffered was the owner of your horse. When I find the money, I'll give it to him."

"Could we have a little chat, maybe? This is coming at me sideways."

"I don't want any more little chats. I want you to stay away from me. All that *stuff* up at your farm, and all the time all you were doing was making sure your tracks were covered. Well, I've uncovered them."

"Look, Lucy, so far I've heard that you've found out that Trimble had put together some crazy rigged bet. Cowan told me. Have a little patience. Let's pretend, anyway. Okay? Pretend I don't know a thing about it. Now tell me what the hell this is all about."

"This is ridiculous."

"Go along with the gag, though, would you?"

"You just want to find out how much I know."

"That I do. Tell me."

Lucy considered. The evidence was on her computer. He couldn't deny that. "All right.

I don't see the point, but I'll go along with the gag, as you say. By the way, what's the name of your horse in tomorrow's race?"

"Up for Grabs. Why?"

"Have you fixed it so he'll win?"

"Watch your mouth, Lucy. He might win, but I think he'll come second or third. Back him to show."

She shrugged. "Did you tell the jockey on —" she glanced at the printout of the race "— Desk Lamp that the horse had been drugged to come last?"

"Keep your voice down, Lucy Brenner. I think you know what you're saying and I'd like you to spell it out. And no more silly questions about my horse, eh? I'm curious. What's up with you?"

"You know perfectly well." She turned away and immediately turned back. "All right. My cousin left a diary behind, one he kept on his computer. There's a lot of stuff on it about the horse that won the race that Desk Lamp was in. A horse called Sly Peek. David had a big bet on it, and he collected his winnings. But then I think David might have been robbed. The diary says that MacGovern, David, you, and a man named Nolan put the swindle together, but you and David double-crossed the others."

"You think we arranged the way that race was going to go?"

"David would never have bet so much if the race hadn't been rigged."

"What do you think I can tell you?"

"Did you make Desk Lamp run slow?"

Now Comstock grew angry. "Lucy. I don't use drugs to make my horses run slow. Not many trainers do. I don't bet; nor does the jockey. He doesn't do dope, either. Ask round. Ask round about me, too. I train horses for fun. I own enough real estate here and in Florida to keep me comfortable for two lives. By and large, the owners come to me because they like my attitude. They trust me. Ask round."

Lucy decided he was angry enough to tell the truth. "Then what happened to Desk Lamp that day?"

"Would you believe me, I don't know. I've already told the stewards that, and the owner. Something got to him. Possibly nothing. It does happen that a horse can't get up for it on a particular day. He struggled along at the back of the field with his tongue hanging out. It's not like him."

"Are you saying he wasn't drugged?"

"The stewards had him tested, so did I. There was no evidence of a drug."

"An unknown drug?"

"It's possible. You hear them brag that they are always a step ahead of the chemists."

"Who would benefit?"

"Your cousin, apparently." Comstock smiled, assuming a tolerant, ironical attitude.

"Could he have got near your horse?"

"I wouldn't have let him or his pals within fifty yards of any horse I train. Your cousin was . . ."

"Bad."

"That's the term," Comstock agreed. "He could have found someone to do it."

"But how could he be sure Sly Peek would win?"

"Now we're coming to it, the flaw in your scenario. He couldn't, without a lot more help than he could have mustered."

Lucy was feeling the ground shift from under her. The conversation seemed to be leaving Johnny out of the swindle. She took out the copy of the race result from her purse. "According to this, you and David and MacGovern and Nolan were in it together. The diary is very clear. You were a part of it."

"You think I've just been soft-soaping you?"

"What else can I think?"

313

Nina started to speak, but Comstock restrained her. He said, "You plan to stay in this business? The deerstalker racket?"

"I told you, yes."

"May I suggest that you don't get too tricky with the psychology? It could backfire. You ask a guy if it's true he's a crook and he's liable to get antsy. There are always some ugly customers around when the stakes are high, but you can't tell by looking at them. Be careful."

"I'm trying to be."

"Good. Now, who else does the diary talk about? MacGovern, you say. I can't vouch for him. I hardly know the guy. Who else?"

"David, Nolan, and the jockey on Sly Peek, Billy Woodhouse."

After a long pause for dramatic emphasis while he looked at Lucy, he said, "Okay. Nina's turn. But first, let me just say that Billy Woodhouse is a born-again Christian. He won't even ride on Sundays, so you can leave him out. I'll arrange for you to meet him if you like, but ask anyone. Ask Peter here."

Now Lucy looked around and began to realize that something serious was happening. She had been concentrating so hard on Johnny that she had not noticed that Peter Tse was standing by the window. Now she

314

said, "What are you doing here? Nina, what's this all about?"

Nina took a printout from her desk and handed it to Lucy.

Lucy glanced at it. "It's the diary, plus the bits about you. I was trying to spare you that." Then, "How did you get this?"

Tse said, "I got it. I broke into your office. I have keys. Remember, I know how to call up the diary. I was with you when you found out."

"So?"

Johnny said, "Cowan came to see me. You have to understand how big that is. He never leaves his office, but he came down to the track to tell me about this story of yours. It's all bullshit, Lucy, but we'll come to that. I decided I had to see the diary so I talked to Peter. He was already worried about you, so it didn't take much persuading to get him to print out the diary. But then we saw the bits about Nina, surrounding the swindle, and it happens that Peter could remember distinctly that Nina had only taken one day off this summer, in May, not June."

"Rubbish. How could he know that?"

Johnny looked at Nina, who looked at Tse, who looked away.

Good God, Lucy thought. *He's* the one

buying Nina's fur coats.

Nina said, "Peter brings me coffee every day on his way in to work. He always knows when I'm not there. He knew that didn't happen in June, so he got me to look at the printout. Those dates aren't real, Lucy. The real date is in the file index. He wrote the whole diary in one day, on June 11."

Johnny said, "He made it up."

Lucy looked over the printout, read again the names of the horses and realized finally what she was reading, realized that if she compared the names with the names of the horses in Trimble's early attempts at fiction, the initials would probably correspond. It was one of the things you were supposed to look for. The revelation made her feel like the victim of a giant practical joke constructed by her cousin to make a fool of her. "Oh, shit," she said. "His stupid fucking novel." She looked up at the faces of the trio watching her. No one was laughing. That was something. "I'm going back to Longborough," she said.

Johnny said, "Could you postpone it for a few days? I've lined up Nolan now. Remember Nolan? I've spent a long time tracking him down. You owe me."

"I can't see him now! There's no point."

"It'd be polite."

"But . . . oh, I suppose so."

"Greenwood tonight. Meet me at the valet parking door. Seven o'clock. Okay?"

"I suppose so."

Chapter 37

If thoroughbred racing is the sport of kings, then harness racing is, or was, the pastime of farmers and small-town people, especially in the Maritimes. Yet Greenwood, it seemed to Lucy, worked much harder than Woodbine at giving its patrons the feeling that they were having an outing. Successfully, too. Lucy chose the valet service to park her car, which brought her to the entrance to the clubhouse, where, instead of the solitary worshipers she had encountered at Woodbine, family parties seemed to be the norm, arriving for a night out as if to the theater.

Johnny was waiting inside the door. "He's here, and there's lots of room in his section. Let's go. Stick to your story. Tell him you know he was a friend of Trimble's, and ask him if he has any anecdotes for that memoir of yours."

"You think I'm writing that memoir now? I hope David's in hell, backing all the losers."

"Were you ever? Wait a couple of years and write your own."

318

"Why do you think Nolan didn't want to see me?"

"He's shy. A lot of people wondered what you were going to put in that memoir. Now, let's go see him."

He guided her up above the dining room, a long glassed-in enclosure overlooking the winning post, and Lucy was again struck with the sense of being at a performance rather than a racetrack. It seemed like a giant dinner theater. Through the windows, she could see some of the performers warming up, trotting briskly around the circuit.

A hostess tried to commandeer them. Comstock said, "We're meeting someone. We'll take a look round first."

"Do you have a reservation?"

"No." The trainer looked at the largely empty dining room below them. "If we spot him, you can probably find us a seat nearby."

He took Lucy's arm, and they climbed to the top row. "Down there," he pointed. "That's Nolan. Two rows down. On the far left."

Lucy looked where he was pointing and felt an attack of vertigo unjustified by the slope of the stands. When she had recovered, she said, "You're sure?"

"You okay? I don't think he's dangerous. I'll come with you."

"No." Lucy pulled hard on his sleeve. "No. I want to talk to him by myself. You keep an eye on me from here."

"He knows you're looking for him, and we still don't really know why he wouldn't talk to you until now. But, okay, go ahead. He won't hurt you. I'll be here."

"I think I know why he didn't want to see me. If I walk along here, I can come down behind him, can't I, so he won't see me coming?"

"See, the seat behind him is empty. You can slip into it and say boo in his ear. Off you go."

Lucy had about three minutes in which to think of her first sentence. Nolan was quite alone, finishing a steak, the *Racing Guide* open beside him.

She lowered herself with as little fuss as possible onto the seat behind him and waited, willing him to look up. When, finally, the bald brown head swiveled upward, she was calm and ready. "Hello, Ben," she said. "Want me to pretend not to know you?"

The Trog lowered his eyes, then looked up and round the enclosure. "Comstock with you?" he asked.

"I've told him to leave us alone unless he sees you trying to kill me."

He smiled, acknowledging her joke. "Why don't you come down here?"

Lucy climbed down onto the seat beside him, taking the opportunity to shake her head at Johnny, who was watching openly now from the end of the row.

"I guess I've blown my cover," Nolan/Tranter said.

"What's your name here?"

"Ben. Still Ben."

"Nolan?"

"That's right."

"Not in the secret service?"

"I'm just a gambler, Lucy."

There was a lot to find out. "Where did you come from? That first night in Longborough?"

"I was on my way to Kawartha Downs and my car broke down. I'd had a good day at Woodbine, so I took it as an omen."

"Why did you tell me all that stuff, Ben?"

"Would you have said yes to a guy who makes his living betting?"

"Probably not, not so quickly."

"I usually drove up after a good day at the track. To you. To celebrate."

"It's a good thing I didn't tell anyone about you."

He looked like a naughty child, but pleased with himself. "Good story though, wasn't it? Our secret."

"It makes me feel like a fool."

"Tranter, Nolan, what's the difference? It's still me, Lucy." He put his hand on her knee.

She brushed it off. It's not the same, she thought. Sleeping with a gambler and maybe a crook. Not the same as providing a safe house for Ben Tranter, secret agent. And Johnny was watching. Something else occurred to her. "The time I hid you for two days. What was that all about? More romancing?"

"Oh, no. I really had to disappear. I owed a guy. That could've been bad without a place to hide. But I raised a little money and he backed off."

So someone had been trying to kill him. That cheered her up. "Why have you been avoiding me, here, in Toronto? Did you know who I was?"

"When you hear someone is looking for you, you always find out who. Then I heard it was Dave's cousin, so I called your office, just to check. You remember someone hanging up a few days ago?"

"I get three or four calls a day from people who hang up when they hear my voice.

David's customers. Did you know him well?"

"Oh, sure. We talked at the track most days. I placed a couple of bets with him."

"A coincidence. You landing on me in Longborough, I mean."

"It wasn't that much of a coincidence. Dave had told me he had a cousin running a bed-and-breakfast in Longborough. I asked the garage, and they knew you."

"And then you came back to Toronto and told David. Did you tell him how good I was in bed?"

"I never said a word, Lucy, I swear. Sure, I planned to, but not when it turned out like that. You were too good to risk. Nah, Lucy, you were my secret, and a very nice one." He tried to take her hand, but she moved away.

"And that's the only reason you didn't want to see me?"

"Why else? But you didn't know who I was, so why were you looking for me?"

Lucy hesitated, then said, lamely, "I thought I'd write a little piece for the paper about David, sort of a memoir. So I wanted to talk to all his friends."

Nolan frowned. "You sure worked a neat one to get to me. What did I matter? There's plenty who knew Dave."

Lucy realized that they were too closely connected for her to be able to keep it up. She took the printout of the swindle out of her purse and showed it to him.

Nolan read it in wonder. "What the hell is this all about? I wasn't even here then. I was in the States. I phoned you."

"That was the time you were after the master spy in upstate New York?"

Nolan blushed, his brown head turning plum. "I can't make any sense of this. Cowan paid out fifty thousand? Did the sky fall? Billy Woodhouse? Oh, for Christ's sake."

"He made it up."

Nolan blinked at her.

"He made it all up afterward. He was trying to write a novel so he was practicing a plot that involved a diary that would be kept on a computer, that his hero would get access to."

"Dave was writing a novel?" Nolan started to grin, looking round to see if there was someone he could share this last best absurdity with. "How'd you find out?"

Lucy explained, taking full credit.

"That's clever. You'll do a lot better in the business than Dave ever did. Have you talked to all the other guys about it?"

"Only Johnny knows it all. Everyone else

thinks I'm writing a memoir."

"Let's get Comstock over here." Nolan waved to the trainer, who walked along the row and slid in behind Lucy.

"You know each other?" he asked.

Nolan patted Lucy's hand. "We're old friends."

Again Lucy carefully withdrew her hand, not meanly, but with a clear signal to Johnny. Comstock leaned back, looked at the pair of them, and raised his eyebrows. "Small world," was all he said, but he looked as if this was as interesting to him as anything else she had told him. "That why you didn't want to see her?"

"None of your business, Comstock." Nolan put the printout beside his plate. "You know all about this. What's Lucy going to do? What are you going to do?"

"Nothing." The trainer explained how easily a false rumor could hurt him.

"Right," Nolan nodded.

"Peter Tse, my landlord. He's been trying to look after me. He knows."

The Trog considered.

"Anyone else?"

"One other person I can trust."

"Not the police?"

"I was going to them last."

"Good." He looked at Comstock.

325

The trainer said, "There's just you, Nolan." He stood up. "I'll leave you to sort it out together." He shook hands with Nolan, said, "Don't keep her too long," and left.

Nolan said, "How about a pact, Lucy. If you hear that someone's telling the story, then you tell Comstock to spread the word about Ben Tranter, secret agent."

"The Trog, secret agent."

"What?"

"That just slipped out. I was thinking of something else."

"No, you weren't. What did you call me? The Frog?" Nolan laughed. "Like, the prince?"

"That's right. You were a prince who turned into a frog. That's how I'll think of you."

"That's all right, then. We can start again. When can I come down to Longborough?"

"I'm moving to Toronto."

"Better. Here. When?"

"No."

"Why not? It's still me. Not so glamorous, but still me." He shook his head. "I'm just being polite. I can see where you're at now." He looked up significantly at the windows of the bar, at the face of Comstock, watching them.

Lucy stood up. "We did have some nice times, Ben," and held out her hand.

"It's a pact, okay?" They shook hands, and Lucy walked up to the bar.

Chapter 38

It took Nina's ear to receive her reaction after the shock of recognition. First she told her the whole foolish story, punishing herself, steeling herself for giggles, then she explained why she would never see The Trog again, even if Johnny disappeared.

"The truth is that I liked sleeping with a liar. It was exciting, and I think it helped the thing itself. You know? Anyway, I have got Johnny. He's not going to go away. Funny. Part of the excitement with Ben was that I never knew when he would appear. I'd open the door one night and there he'd be . . ."

"I thought you said he always phoned first."

"Okay. I'd pick up the phone and there he would be. Now, there's no reason why he shouldn't come by every Tuesday and Thursday. I don't want that. It would be like an aerobics class."

"A lot of people our age would give their teeth for a trog. Even one who bets. He's not James Bond, but in the real world he still looks pretty good. Especially if you only see him when he's had a good day at the track."

"I suppose. Make a good pal, wouldn't he? I'll see."

"Take your time, Lucy. A good trog is hard to find."

"No. I'm not serious. I don't need him now. Not like that. No. I really only needed him the first time. It's all connected, don't you see? Step one, I left Geoffrey, and Kingston. The Trog came along and saying yes to him was the next step, and my first one out of Longborough. When David died I was ready to leave Longborough. Fate. I'm well away from Longborough now and light-years from Kingston and Geoffrey. Like the girl at the end of the play, I'm free, Nina, I'm free. The Trog was important once; he isn't now. Anyway . . ."

"Anyway, you've got the horseman. So what's next? You going to join the police?"

"Oh, no. I feel a fool about this, but I haven't given the detecting a real try yet. I think I'll like it. Who knows who is going to walk through the door? Oh, no. I'll be here for a while. I've still got another case to finish."

"Mrs. Lindberg?"

"Right. It's Thursday. Are you with me?"

"I wouldn't miss it for the world."

She put her own car in the garage and walked across the street to where Nina was to pick her up. When Nina arrived, they waited outside the back door of the Chicken Chalet for the woman to emerge.

This time she drove south on Yonge Street, all the way down to the lake, and turned into the Queen's Quay parking lot. She's gaining confidence, Lucy thought, glum that it could be just as much a sign that her agoraphobia was improving as a sign that her wings were getting stronger. They circled the lot until the woman had gone through the south door of the building, then parked next to her, on the grounds that once Lucy had approached her there would be no need to hide.

"Together?" Nina asked.

"Why not? That was your idea, wasn't it? We *are* together. Friends from Detroit."

Harbourfront is an old sugar warehouse converted into a swank shopping "concourse" mostly catering to visitors from out of town. As the two women walked through the door by Spinnaker's Restaurant, they spotted her four yards away, window-shopping. Lucy dug her fingers into Nina's arm and pulled her into the foyer of the restaurant. Nina squawked slightly at the pressure

330

of Lucy's nails, and two men at a table in the corner looked up. Lucy was shocked to realize that she knew one of the men very well and nearly waved until she realized that the man was famous and that she knew him only from his picture on the jacket of a dozen crime novels. "My God," she said, forgetting her purpose for the moment. "That's Clive Sparrow."

"Who?"

"Clive Sparrow. He's a mystery writer, from England. What's he doing here?"

"Who's that with him?"

A shortish, solid-looking character with not much hair and glasses. "I don't know him. Looks like his bodyguard."

The waiter approached them. Nina shook her head and pulled Lucy out of the restaurant and across the hall, where they could see that the woman on her side had made hardly any progress.

"There is something odd going on," Nina said. "She's spent five minutes looking at the curtains in that restaurant window. There isn't even a menu. Now look at her."

The woman had stopped now, and was looking behind her.

"She's looking for someone," Nina said.

"Me. She's looking for me. Let's just make sure. Leave me alone. I'm going to let her see me, then disappear. Watch her. See what happens. She's looking for someone alone. The two of us fooled her. Thank God you're here."

Nina glided off and took up a position by a pillar fifteen yards away. Lucy crossed the aisle and began moving along the row of windows toward her quarry. The woman disappeared around the corner of the shops, and Lucy turned back and made her way on the outside of the crowd to Nina.

Nina shifted her weight onto the other leg. "You need lessons to stand about inconspicuously," she said. "I feel like Marlene Dietrich playing a hooker. You know, *Underneath the Lamplight*, only with a bigger bum."

"Where is she now?"

"She hasn't moved. Look at her."

Once more the woman was revolving slowly, without doubt now looking for someone following her.

"I don't like this," Lucy said.

"Don't worry, Nina's here. Now let's go home and I'll tell you what's going on."

"Home?"

"Somewhere." Nina urged her out of the building.

Lucy allowed herself to be carried off to the car. "Where now?"

"Somewhere quiet. Somewhere near the garage. Let's eat something. I'll tell you when I've had a drink."

Lucy held her tongue until they reached Browne's Bistro, where, over a shared lamb sausage pizza, Nina told her what was going on.

She waited in her office the next morning until eleven o'clock for Lindberg to appear. She had asked Peter Tse to leave his door open and listen, and across the street Nina sat close to the window ready to dash over if she saw Lucy in any trouble. There was no apparent reason why he should be violent, but it was unfamiliar ground, and it was best to be prepared for anything.

By eleven o'clock he was evidently not coming, apparently having decided that his weekly jolly would have to be managed in front of someone other than Lucy in future. He had obviously drawn the right conclusion from Lucy's flight. She wondered who he would get next time, who "would do." She added up the account and figured that she owed him fifty dollars, if he ever came to collect.

"It was the picture," Nina had said the

evening before as she drank her wine. "There was something phony about it from the start, that bothered me. If you look at it again you can see he probably took it himself with a timer."

"I'm no good at this job."

"Don't be silly. I have expert knowledge. I married one."

"A . . . ?"

"Transvestite, honey. Call them cross-dressers. My husband only did it at home, but that was enough for me when I came home early one day."

Nina's revelation made Lucy feel she had straw in her hair, not because of its content, but in the casual way Nina had lifted up the corner of her otherwise mysterious private life. Nobody in Longborough had talked about transvestites, not to her, anyway, but then Nina's secret, if that's what it was, wouldn't have lasted five minutes in Longborough. Lucy forced herself to stop staring at Nina.

"Should I tell the police?" she asked.

"Why? It's not illegal. It's not even a big deal. There are thousands of them around, even in Longborough. There are degrees, I guess, but most are satisfied to totter about on high heels behind closed curtains. Harmless enough. He paid you fifty an hour for the thrill of fooling you. He got his money's worth."

"I'll say. He got the right one, didn't he?"

Could what Nina was saying be true? About transvestites in Longborough. Was she that naïve? Maybe the ladies of her book club were protecting her. Surely not. Surely it was just an odd gap in her knowledge, like not knowing how to pronounce "idyll."

There remained the glasses, but not for long. Brighton called to say he had discovered the owner, and promised to drop the glasses off with the owner's name later in the day. He delivered them within the hour, preserving the mystery of why he wanted her to meet him later in the week at Yuk-Yuk's. It was important, he said, but he couldn't say why until that night.

When he had gone, she cleared the front half of her desk and placed the glasses in the cleared space as if in a window display. When Tse came in he saw them immediately.

"My spare glasses. Jesus. Where'd you find them? I've been searching for them all over. They cost me four hundred bucks."

"The people at the morgue had them. The

ambulance attendant found them by David. The police assumed they had fallen out of his pocket."

"They must have fallen out when I tried to help him. That's terrific." Now Tse looked at her. "What's the matter? Why are you looking at me like that?" Then, "You put them out for me to see, didn't you? You've had them all along. When did you know they were mine?"

"Today."

Tse looked at her, down at the desk, then back up to her face. "Lucy. You thought they might have belonged to the guy you thought killed him, didn't you?"

"I knew they weren't David's. They're the wrong strength, and he would never wear bifocals."

"No, he wouldn't. Clever. Clever. Oh, Lucy, you silly bitch." He threw back his head and laughed to show where he was coming from, that it was a term of endearment. "And what happened about that woman you were following?"

"Can we go somewhere for coffee? I'll tell you the rest of it."

After three sentences in the Portuguese café, Tse was grinning, and at the end he was bouncing in his seat with glee. Then he got control of himself and patted Lucy's hand. "Never mind," he said. "You've done wonders."

"I've made a complete cake of myself."

"No, you haven't. It was clever of you to find out who owned my glasses."

"Jack Brighton did that."

"It was *your* idea. I think you're suited to the business."

"Jack thinks so, too."

"There you are, then. You can have the same rent as Dave."

The next day Cowan, the bookmaker, called. After two or three sentences in which he made it clear there was nothing more to be said about Trimble the novelist, he said, "Have you had any of David's customers wanting to invest with you?"

"Three or four a day."

"What have you told them?"

"The truth. David's dead, and the betting business has moved."

"I wondered if you'd given any thought to it yourself?"

"Me? Hey, do I look like a bookie's runner?"

"That's an English expression, I think. I've never heard it over here. I can see you might not feel comfortable. If you change your mind, though, you know where to find me."

"Not me, Mr. Cowan. I'm staying away from gamblers."

"It's just a living, Mrs. Brenner."

They drove past the Dentons' farm four times, every half-hour, until she saw that the truck had gone. Then she telephoned the farm from a call box on the highway. Nora Denton answered and confirmed that Denton had gone to Toronto. Ten minutes later, Lucy was in the farmhouse and telling Mrs. Denton of the legacy, explaining that she had made sure no news of it would come to the farmhouse without Nora Denton's consent. "All you have to do is tell me where you want the money deposited," she said.

"It's a lot of money."

"It's yours."

"Maybe if I give him half? I could make a start again on the rest."

"The money is yours."

"He'd come after me."

"Tell the police. Go to the shelter in Longborough. Tell them."

"Could I stay there?"

"I think so. For a few days."

"Then what?"

Lucy had wanted to avoid this, but she

felt committed. "Don't you have anyone in Longborough? Or Toronto?"

"I couldn't go to Toronto. I wouldn't know where to go to feel safe. And there's only his relatives in Longborough. I got a brother out west someplace, that's all."

Lucy looked around the appalling room. "You could stay in my house until you get sorted out. There's plenty of room."

"I could help you out," the woman said quickly, following her glance. "I don't like to live like this."

Lucy had her doubts. "Just until you get organized. We'll get you a lawyer and find out your rights."

"When shall I come?"

"Now. Before he gets back."

Fifteen minutes later the woman came downstairs with a suitcase and three plastic bags of clothes. "Quick. Let's go," she said. "I won't even leave a note. That way it'll take him more time to find me."

Lucy went to the door and waved, and Johnny brought the car up close, said something to the dog that sent it scuttling, its lips in place, and loaded them in. Lucy gave him the address and they drove north, straight to Lucy's house.

Back in the city, Lucy phoned Mrs. Tibbles to tell her what she'd done.

"That sounds splendid. But Denton is bound to find her. What's your address in Longborough? I'll have the police keep an eye on the house, frighten him off. I still know the chief. By the way, Henry and I discussed your involvement, and I've sent you a check. A sort of retainer."

"You want me to work for you?'

"Yes, although I don't have anything for you to do at the moment."

"I see. You want to know of anything more I might hear that could affect you."

"Yes."

"All right."

It was five thousand dollars. Not a bribe, Lucy reminded herself. A retainer.

Yuk-Yuk's was more crowded than before. It was amateur night again. Lucy found a seat near the back and waited for Brighton to join her. She kept a seat for Johnny, who was coming later. She was halfway through her beer when Brighton came out on stage. He told about a dozen jokes, some of which were genuinely funny, and retired to a good round of applause.

"Jack Brighton, secret comic," she said, when he appeared at her table.

"How was I?"

"They like you. This is why you asked me to come? Me and all the others?"

There was a steady stream of well-wishers at their table, steady enough to make Lucy realize that Brighton had papered the house.

"I need all the help I can get. Couple more nights like this and I might get paid. Or run out of friends."

"Good luck." Lucy finished her beer.

"Don't run away. I've got something for you."

"A job. I don't need any more surprises."

"There's a bookshop that's being lifted too much. They want a store detective for a day, someone like you. They think it must be one of their regular customers. They'd like to know who before they do anything. It could be embarrassing for them."

"What do I do?"

"You spend the day browsing."

"Fifty an hour?"

"Two hundred for the day. If you catch them early you still get your two hundred."

"All right. Why don't you do it?"

"I don't know how to browse. Besides, I've got an audition Saturday. For a paid job."

"What's the name of the store?"

Brighton told her, adding, "There's a second show here tonight."

Johnny said, in her ear, "My sides are aching from the first show. Let's go."

That night, Comstock said, "Will you marry me, Lucy?"

"Just so that I can't testify against you?"

"That, too."

She pushed him off, onto his back, then hauled herself up until her head was level with his. "No," she said, finally.

"You could forget about Trimble's agency. I'll look after you."

"No."

"Is there something wrong with me?"

"No."

"Then why, for God's sake?"

"Because I don't need anyone to look after me. I didn't come all this way just to get married again, even to you, though I do love you."

"How will I introduce you to my mother?"

"You can tell her I'm your latest, and I'll tell her you're mine."

Finally, the police called to tell her they had found the persons who had broken into her office. They had conducted a raid on premises occupied by three Vietnamese youths, and come across a hoard of stolen goods. Trimble's binoculars were among them, identifiable by a customs declaration inside the case.

A week later Johnny helped her with her last problem. He put his head round the door to take her to lunch.

She looked at the list in front of her. "Trimble Investigations; L. Trimble, Private Investigator; Lucy Trimble, Private Investigator. Which?"

"Why are you using his name still?"

"It's *my* name, too. Brenner was my old name, my married name."

"Then 'Lucy Trimble.' "

"Why?"

"I like it. Now let's eat."

We hope you have enjoyed this Large Print book. Other Thorndike Press or Chivers Press Large Print books are available at your library or directly from the publishers.

For more information about current and upcoming titles, please call or write, without obligation, to:

Thorndike Press
P.O. Box 159
Thorndike, Maine 04986 USA
Tel. (800) 223-2336

OR

Chivers Press Limited
Windsor Bridge Road
Bath BA2 3AX
England
Tel. (0225) 335336

All our Large Print titles are designed for easy reading, and all our books are made to last.